DARK STRANGER

STRANGER immortal

THE CHILDREN OF
THE GODS 3

I. T. LUCAS

INTERNATIONALLY BESTSELLING AUTHOR

Dark Stranger Immortal is a work of fiction!

Names, characters, places and incidents are products of the author's imagination or are used fictitiously and are not to be construed as real. Any similarity to actual persons, organizations and/or events is purely coincidental.

Published by Evening Star Press

EveningStarPress.com

ISBN: 978-1-957139-21-0

DARK STRANGER IMMORTAL

THE CHILDREN OF THE GODS BOOK 3

I. T. LUCAS

PREVIOUSLY: AMANDA

"We need to talk," Amanda said as soon as she entered Kian's office.

Scowling, he eased back in his chair and folded his arms across his chest.

If he thought he could intimidate her with this angry scowl of his, he had another thing coming. Halting in front of his desk, she placed her hands on her hips and began tapping her shoe. "What did you do to her this time?"

Uncrossing his arms, Kian placed his palms on the glossy surface of his desk and pinned her with a hard stare. "What do you want, Amanda?" he barked.

Amanda winced. Shit, she had done it again. When would she learn that coming at Kian with her proverbial guns blazing would get her nowhere? She'd better change her tone quickly before he kicked her out without hearing what she had to say.

Plopping down on the chair facing him, she forced a milder tone. "Syssi is upset and unhappy. You must've either done something or said something to hurt her."

His expression changing from angry to frustrated, Kian ran his fingers through his hair. "I know. But I'll be damned if I know what it was. I hoped she would tell you."

So he knew he had done something wrong. Amanda frowned and straightened in her chair. "Syssi told me she was overwhelmed with all the stuff she had to wrap her mind around, but I know there is more to it. The way she was holding her arms around her middle she seemed almost in physical pain." Watching him carefully, Amanda searched his face for signs of guilt. If the idiot had let loose and been too rough with Syssi, she was going to... what? Hire some goons to rough him up? Well, she would think of something...

He winced, and for a moment, she suspected the worst. But then he shook his head. "No, she was fine after we... After we made love... It was only after I told her our story that she clammed up."

Amanda released the breath she'd been holding. If it had been only his clumsy delivery that had upset Syssi, then things were not as bad as she'd suspected. Although Fates only knew how Kian had managed to bungle things up, and if there was anything left for her to salvage.

"Tell me everything exactly as it happened. You may not know what you've done wrong, but I might."

"Everything?" Kian cocked his brow with a little smile tugging at his lips.

Amanda waved a hand in front of her face. "Ugh! I don't need the steamy details! Too much information, just the sequence of events, please, and what you said to her, or rather how you said it. We both know you tend to be somewhat uncouth." To call his style uncouth was the understatement of the millennia, but she knew she had to tread lightly if she wanted him to cooperate.

Kian sighed. "Okay. So last night after we came back from the club, I didn't thrall her after the sex. She was spacey from the bite, and I figured it was the perfect time to tell her what was going on, while she was still in a receptive mood and wouldn't freak out. It just didn't feel right to keep thralling her and lying to her. I decided to come clean the way we did with Michael. I told her some of it last night and the rest this morning. She didn't freak out, didn't panic, but she got upset. Mainly because she figured out that I would have to erase her memory if she didn't turn. But then she seemed to understand why it was necessary and seemed better, then got upset again and wouldn't tell me why."

"Tell me exactly how you explained it to her."

"Why?"

"Just humor me, I have a feeling your presentation lacked finesse, and since I wasn't there, the only way I can figure it out is to hear it word for word."

"I told her everything, pretty much the same way we explained it to Michael. Our history, the unique biology, how important both Michael and she might be to the future of our clan. Then I elaborated a little more about the venom and how it works. The first time she really got upset was when she realized she'd be sent away if she didn't turn. The second was when I explained about the possibility of her getting addicted to the venom. Instead of alleviating her concerns, the more I explained how it could be circumvented by having several different partners, the more cold and distant she became. I think I did my best to make it clear that if she were to turn, she wasn't trapped in a relationship with me because of it and would be free to choose anyone she wanted."

Kian's face twisted with rage. "And believe me, it cost me to get the words out of my mouth," he growled.

She knew Kian was on the verge of exploding, but she just couldn't help herself. "Suave, Kian... really suave, almost two thousand years old and clueless." Amanda shook her head, she was blowing it. Maybe a little flattery would placate him. "I'm amazed that an intelligent and experienced man like you can be so blind."

"That's enough, Amanda! I will not tolerate this tone of voice from you. You're my sister and I love you, but that doesn't mean I'll allow you to talk to me with disrespect." Kian's rage found an outlet, but it had been a mild explosion.

If he thought she would cower before him, he had forgotten who he was dealing with. Amanda bowed her head with mock penitence. "My apologies, Regent, you're right of course. This era is not very respectful toward its elders." She smirked.

Her little jibe worked. Kian looked at her sternly, but a smile was tugging at his lips. "You're forgiven. Now talk... respectfully..."

Okay, I can do respectful...

3

Amanda straightened her back and clasped her hands before her on Kian's desk. Affecting her teacher's voice, she asked, "How do you feel about Syssi? Think about it for a moment before you answer. I want you to get a clear picture in your head."

Kian didn't take long. "She is sweet. I like how unassuming she is. She is definitely smart, and not prone to dramatics or exaggerations like some people I know..." He looked at her pointedly, and she rolled her eyes. "Syssi is beautiful, lush, sensual... lustful... I can't get enough of her, and she responds in kind... We are definitely in serious lust with each other." Kian smiled, then took in a hissed breath.

"Are you sure it's only lust?" Amanda probed gently.

"What else could it be? We've known each other for less than four days..." Avoiding Amanda's eyes, Kian once again raked his fingers through his messed-up hair.

"So you didn't become a jealous monster when another male was sniffing around her, or turn practically demonic just at the thought of her with another guy?" Amanda asked with a smug smile.

Bracing his elbows on the desk, Kian dropped his head on his fists. "I did. Big time." He sighed. "I was ready to pound Anandur to a pulp, and barely held myself from breaking Alex's arm when the scumbag touched her. I don't know what came over me. I've never been the jealous type, not even with Lavena, whom I loved... had a child with... I don't understand what's happening to me."

Poor guy, he has no idea...

"Yet you've told Syssi that she is important *to the clan*, that she should not fear addiction because she can choose *some other male* for her mate."

Kian's anger flared anew. "So? It's true! I wanted her to know she is important to us, and I didn't want her to feel trapped or forced. She has the right to know what her options are."

Amanda palmed his tightly fisted hand and held it in both of hers. "You lied, Kian; lied to yourself, lied to Syssi, and by doing so you hurt both of you," she said in a somber tone to drive the point home.

Kian tried to pull away from her, but she held on. "Listen to me! She is important to *you*, and you want her to choose *you* because you want her for *yourself,* not for the clan. That's what she wanted to hear, needed you to say, and it also happens to be the truth."

When he didn't try to refute this, she continued, "Syssi is not like us. She is not someone who has casual sex. This thing with you means the world to her. The poor girl had just one lover until now and went without sex for two years, for goodness' sake… And the way you explained things made her feel like she is nothing to you… Way to go, Kian…" With a last disapproving look, she finally let go of Kian's hand.

"I'm an ass…" Kian dropped his head and rubbed at his temples.

"I'm such a moron…"

"No, my dear, sweet brother, you're not a moron, just inexperienced; shagging thousands of women notwithstanding. You don't know how to deal with your own emotions, let alone someone else's. You've never had to woo a female so you don't know how to go about it. But all is not lost. I'll help you romance her back." Amanda squared her shoulders, pushing her chin up.

Kian chuckled. "You, Amanda? What do you know about wooing or romance? What do any of us know? We use and discard partners like dirty underwear or used condoms."

"Okay, Kian, now you're being crude. As regent, you're not allowed."

He dismissed her with a wave of his hand. "In here, I'm just your brother."

"Could have fooled me… Watch your tone, Amanda… I demand respect, Amanda…" She emulated his haughty tone, crossing her arms over her chest and jutting her chin out.

"Cut the crap. What do you suggest I do, Miss Know-It-All?"

"I do have some human female friends, and I've read a few romance novels, so I do have some idea of what mortal females want—besides the shagging, or in addition to it, that is. You should take her out on a date, make it several dates, to some classy, romantic restaurant, or a show, the theater. Take her dancing. And gifts—I think mortal females expect that from their suitors. Shower her with attention, but it has to be outside the bed… or the wall… or the closet… or the shower…" True to her nature, Amanda couldn't help herself and kept going. But he just smirked. "Make her feel she is the most important person in the world to you. Tell her how you feel, show her; give yourself to her and make her yours." Amanda sighed. How she longed for a man to become as enamored with her as Kian was with Syssi. But what were the chances of that? None.

"But what if she is not compatible, and I have to let her go, erase her memories? It's going to hurt like hell…"

"Letting her go is going to hurt like hell regardless of what you do. You're already head over heels with her. But, at least this way, giving it all, letting this thing between you bloom, you'll get to sample a little bit of wonderful. The consequences of not admitting the truth and following your heart would bring a whole new world of hurt, much worse than just letting her go." She shivered. "I hate to think what that would do to you."

"What do you mean? What could be worse?"

Seriously? Did Kian have no imagination at all?

"What could be worse? Think of it this way; she turns immortal, but wants nothing to do with you, chooses another male… one you cannot kill because they are all your nephews."

"You're right. That is worse…" His eyes flashed dangerously as what she had said sunk in. Agitated, he pushed out of his chair and began pacing the length of his office.

"Take a risk, Kian. I have a really good feeling about Syssi, Michael too." Amanda's eyes followed Kian as he paced back and forth.

"You've had good feelings before and see how well those turned out," he said sarcastically, stopping to glare down at her.

"This time it's different. You didn't react like that to the others, as a matter of fact, with anyone… And besides, I was just reminded of a talk I had with Mother a couple of months back. She said something I didn't pay attention to at the time, but I think you'll find it intriguing. You know how she sometimes makes those cryptic remarks that do not make any sense at the time, but then are crystal clear in hindsight?"

"What did she say?"

"She called me. We talked about my research, and she said, 'Finally you found what the soul eternally craves.' I thought she just misused the language—you know, the way she sometimes translates from her native tongue and it comes out weird. I thought what she meant was that I'd found my heart's desire—something I like to do. But thinking back, she didn't say *your soul,* she said *the soul,* meaning that I'd found something not for me personally but in general. What do all of our souls eternally crave, Kian?" Amanda looked into her brother's eyes.

"A mate—an immortal, truelove mate," Kian said quietly.

"Bingo!"

1

KIAN

The silence that followed was interrupted by Okidu's light knock on the door. "Master, Dr. Bridget is here to see you."

Tearing his gaze away from his sister's hopeful face, Kian frowned. Amanda was so excited, her deep blue eyes were glowing. Unfortunately, she was reading too much into their mother's words, grasping for meaning where there was none.

In his opinion, false hope was more dangerous than the baser emotions people scorned. A cruel and powerful mistress, hope obscured common sense and made random occurrences appear as meaningful signs, prompting those who followed its misleading trail to take questionable actions. Mindlessly disregarding the well-being of others and their own sense of self-preservation for hope's illusive promise, more often than not, they were rewarded by nothing but chaos and pain.

"Show her in," he told Okidu. "On second thought, never mind. I'll go to her."

In the living room, Bridget was pacing the small distance between the front door and the edge of the rug, looking agitated.

Great. His lips pulled into a tight line. Another female ready to tear into him over something he had supposedly done wrong.

Take a number and stand in line.

"Good afternoon, Bridget, what a nice surprise." Kian wondered if she heard the thinly veiled sarcasm in his tone.

The doctor wrung her hands nervously. "Good afternoon, Kian, sorry to come up here without calling ahead, but this is urgent."

"Think nothing of it. No one else does." He placed his hand on her shoulder, conveying the reassurance his tone didn't. "What can I do for you, Bridget?"

"I've just learned that you have two potential Dormants here, and frankly, I was appalled I had to hear it from William. How come you didn't check with me before initiating the process? I need blood samples before and after each venom injection. This is the first time I've had adult Dormants who I could test as we are attempting to activate them, and there might be a chance that their blood will provide the clues I need. You know how important this is." By the time she finished her rant, her temper had painted her cheeks red to match the color of her hair.

"You're right. With everything that was going on, it didn't even cross my mind. But my oversight aside, I don't want you to get your hopes up. I don't believe they are really what we are looking for, but just in case..."

"Yeah, just in case... Hi, Bridget." Amanda gave the petite woman a hug. "Don't listen to him, he of little faith. They. Are. It," she whispered in the doctor's ear, making sure it was loud enough for Kian to hear.

He rolled his eyes. "I'll make sure they'll be at your lab shortly."

"Thank you." Bridget smiled a tight, nervous smile and hurried out.

Closing the door behind her, Kian turned to Amanda. "I assume Syssi is at your place?"

"She is in my office. I've had her sit down to do some work."

"Good, I'll get her. Call for someone to escort Michael to the lab, unless you want to do it yourself?"

They walked out together.

"Remember! Be nice... Woo her!" Amanda slapped his back before punching the button for the elevator.

Woo her, right.

What the hell did that mean? Kian wracked his brain trying to come up with something that would qualify as wooing. Should he quote poetry? He chuckled. He didn't know any. Didn't like it, and in his opinion, it was a lot of pretentious crap. If one wanted to convey an idea, one ought to do it in a way that would be clearly understood and not mask it in vague wording. Whatever. His opinion on poetry notwithstanding, he needed something more concrete than that word.

Woo.

Being serious and pragmatic wasn't going to help him woo anyone, besides business associates, that is, not that he was any good at that either. Kian thought of himself as courteous and polite, and he was... most of the time... unless his temper got the better of him. Other than that, the extent of his social skills was limited to business dealings and seducing women in bars and clubs.

It wasn't much to work with. In comparison, even bloody Anandur seemed like a witty charmer.

I'm so screwed...

With his footfalls making almost no sound on the hallway's soft rug, Syssi didn't hear his approach. She didn't even lift her head when he peered into Amanda's office.

For a moment, he observed her unawares. She looked adorable; scrunching her little nose in concentration, her wild multicolor hair all over the place—cascading down her back and front, covering her left breast while leaving the other outlined perfectly against her white, low-necked T-shirt.

She was so damn sexy it hurt.

Did she wear those T-shirts on purpose to taunt him? How was he supposed to get his head out of the gutter when she looked so tempting? Kian heaved a sigh. It would be next to impossible to follow Amanda's advice and interact with Syssi in a nonsexual way.

She looked up from her work. "Hi, Kian... What was the heavy sigh for?"

For a moment there, he was tempted to yank her out of her chair and show her. Instead, he raked his itchy fingers through his hair. "Bridget, our in-house doctor, wants to take some blood samples from you and Michael. She needs to run tests before and after each venom infusion..."

On the wooing scale of one to ten, that was probably a minus two.

With an inward curse, Kian's brows drew tight. "Come, she is waiting for us in her lab." He offered his hand.

Yep, I'm Mr. Fucking Debonair.

2

SYSSI

There he goes again. Syssi winced.

In a heartbeat, Kian went from looking wistful to grumpy, his darkening mood casting an unpleasant, oppressive shadow.

Syssi swallowed past the hard lump in her throat. Was he suddenly reminded of the dismissive way she had treated him before?

Okay... two could play that game. She could be aloof and grumpy as well...

Yeah right...

Holding onto Kian's hand as they headed for the elevator, Syssi struggled just to keep herself from plastering her body against his and rubbing all over him—like a cat on a scratching post.

But a quick glance at his grim, agitated face was enough to kill that impulse.

As they stood side by side, waiting for the elevator, there was an awkward silence between them, and if not for his hand holding onto hers almost crushingly, she would've thought he didn't want to be with her.

As soon as the doors slid shut behind them, the tension got even worse. With the memory of last night's momentous ride slamming down hard, the already small space shrunk around her, constricting her air supply.

"Fuck that!" Was all the warning she got before Kian shoved her against the wall and smashed his lips over hers with a low guttural sound reverberating deep in his throat. He held her in place with his hand on her nape, his tongue invading her welcoming mouth.

She moaned.

Her small needy whimpers must've urged him on, and he bent his knees to align their bodies, gyrating his hips and grinding himself against her.

Testing, she pushed her tongue past his lips and thrust into his mouth. He let her, groaning as she went on swirling and licking at his fangs' extended length.

"More…" Kian growled when she left his mouth to kiss and nip at his throat, pulling her back to his lips, "… my fangs, I never knew it'd feel so damn good…"

Was she the first to give him this pleasure? Floored by his admission, Syssi's heart swelled with satisfaction. Kissing him long and hard, she swirled her tongue round and round his fangs until he groaned with bliss.

Once again, they were on fire, their need for each other insatiable. But unlike last night, acting on it was not an option. As the elevator chime announced that it'd reached its destination, Kian released her, and a moment later she let go of him as well.

Panting breathlessly as Kian held the door from closing, Syssi took a moment to compose herself before exiting into the wide corridor.

"Hold on!" He grabbed her arm as she stepped out. "I need another moment here." He leaned his back against the hallway's wall, holding onto her bicep as if afraid she'd bolt. "Between my fangs and what's going on down below, I'll make quite a spectacle of myself if I walk into Bridget's lab like this."

"Need me to talk about gross, disgusting stuff? I can help you deflate in no time…" Syssi giggled, not at all sorry for his predicament.

Kian cocked a brow. "What gross stuff?"

"Once, when I was at the mall, I saw this little kid in a stroller eating a hamburger. He choked on a larger piece and puked, but kept eating the puke-covered hamburger as if nothing happened. Meanwhile, his mother was chatting with a friend and pushing the stroller, bewildered by the horror-filled glances of passers-by, oblivious to what was happening, until a saleslady ran out from one of the stores with a roll of paper towels."

Kian chuckled. "Only you could think of telling a story like that. I was expecting guts and gore, and here you go, talking about little kids and puke." He caressed her cheek tenderly. "My sweet Syssi." He bent to kiss the top of her head.

"But it worked, didn't it?" She smirked.

"Yep, only partially, but it will do. Let's go." He took her hand and led her toward the lab.

Whatever it was that had him all twisted up before seemed to have ebbed, and Kian was once again affectionate and easygoing with her. She wondered if their kiss in the elevator had been responsible for Kian's mood change.

Yeah, that was probably it.

Smiling up at him, she asked, "You know the saying that the way to a man's heart is through his stomach?"

"What about it?"

She joggled her brows. "In your case, it's not the stomach."

"I have a newsflash for you, baby…" Kian snorted. "Unless a guy is gay or impotent or otherwise compromised, I don't care who he is; sex would always trump a full stomach." Pulling her tightly against his side, he gave a little squeeze.

As they walked into the lab, Bridget was tying a rubber tube around Michael's bicep. Sitting on one of the metal tables, Michael winced and turned his head away. "I hate needles, can you make it quick, Doctor?"

"Don't be a big baby. You're just like my son. Watching gory horror movies that make me cover my eyes and ears is fine, but a drop of his own blood makes him faint." Bridget plunged the needle in one swift move.

Syssi sat on the table beside him. "Hi, Michael, how are you feeling?" She took his right hand to distract him from what was going on with his left.

"Nauseous… faint…" he admitted with a grimace.

"I mean, how are you feeling after the match, anything hurt?" She kept talking, drawing his attention to herself and away from the needle and the number of glass vials Bridget was filling with his blood.

"Oh, that? Nah, it's all good. That venom is a miracle drug. Most of the bruises were gone in a couple of hours, and the pains and aches even before that. I wish I had the stuff after football practice or games, or when…"

As he kept talking, Bridget finished filling the vials. "All done, big boy, you can hop down now." She removed the tourniquet and pressed a gauze square to the crook of his arm, attaching it with an adhesive tape. "Want a lollypop?"

"Sure, I'd love one. What flavors you got?"

"Cherry, apple, and caramel."

"I'll take the apple. Is it sour?"

"I don't know…" She smiled. "Here you go." She handed him two apple-flavored lollypops.

"It's your turn, young lady. How is your relationship with needles?" Bridget finished sticking labels on the tubes she had filled with Michael's blood and pulled out a new tourniquet to tie around Syssi's bicep.

"Don't love them, don't hate them… I'm not squeamish." Syssi held out her arm.

Michael walked over to where Kian was leaning against another lab table and eased back beside him. Sucking on his pop, he offered Kian his spare one. "Want a pop?"

"No, I'm good, kid. Keep it for later."

"So, Doctor Bridget, what exactly are you going to do with all that blood?" Michael asked, waving the pop in the direction of the test-tube rack.

"Well, I'm going to run a bunch of tests. Genetic tests mostly. First I'm going to check your mitochondrial DNA to establish your matrilineal descent and make sure you and Syssi are not from the same line, or ours. Then I'm going to be checking for anything and everything that might give me a clue. Unfortunately, the knowledge rescued from the cataclysm did not include medicine or genetics, so we are just as clueless as mortals on those subjects." She sighed, placing another ampule of Syssi's blood in the rack.

Alarmed by the possibility, Syssi glanced at Kian. By the grim expression on his face, so was he. "Is there a chance we might be of the same line as you guys?" she asked.

"It's a very remote chance. Annani was an only daughter to her mother, who was also an only daughter. The gods started mating with mortals only after Annani's mother came of age and not before. So as far as we know, there weren't any other descendants from that line besides Annani. But we need to make sure. We take the taboos very seriously. In-line mating might have disastrous genetic implications that we couldn't even fathom. As

15

promiscuous as the gods were, there must have been a good reason for such a strong taboo."

"Well, let's hope for the best. I'm positive you'll find Michael and I are from two completely different lines..." Syssi smiled, trying to reassure Kian, or maybe herself.

"Yes, I certainly hope so." Bridget finished with the last test tube.

"Hope springs eternal for the young and naive. Personally, I hate the bitch," Kian spat as he pushed away from the table. "In my experience, hope is often groundless. Fairy tales have happy endings—real life seldom does." He lifted Syssi off the table as if the one-foot jump down could be hazardous to her health, or perhaps just used it as an excuse to hold her tightly for a moment.

Whatever his reasons for the gallant gesture, at the contact her skin prickled with awareness. And as he held her close, she breathed in his unique musk, getting intoxicated by it. Syssi had to briefly close her eyes. The man smelled absolutely delicious. When he reluctantly released her, she opened her eyes slowly, swaying on her feet a little before turning to Bridget. "When will you have something for us?"

Fidgeting with her equipment, the doctor seemed uneasy with their open display of affection. "The mitochondrial DNA testing will be done probably today. The rest will take as long as it does. I have a slew of tests I'm thinking of, and probably will come up with some more as I go."

"Don't you need to send it out to a genetics lab?" Syssi didn't know what exactly was required, but the small lab they were in certainly didn't have anything looking even remotely sophisticated.

"Oh, this?" Bridget followed Syssi's appraising eyes. "This is just my examination room. I have all the best equipment available in the lab proper, a level down from here. Besides this room, I also have an operating room and several recovery rooms. I'm a whole hospital and research facility of one." Her chin went up. "I have everything a girl like me could ever dream of." She blew a kiss at Kian. "All thanks to our very generous regent."

"Flattery will get you everywhere." Kian blew her a kiss back. "You'll let us know as soon as you have the initial results?"

"You'll be the first to know," Bridget promised.

As they made their way back to the elevator, Michael was a step behind them. "Do you guys really need to keep me locked up? Can't I at least enjoy the freedom of the basement? Syssi gets to, so why can't I?"

Michael seemed to be happy and excited about the opportunity he had been given, and Syssi doubted he would bolt. But apparently, Kian wasn't ready to take the risk.

He glanced back at Michael, appraising him.

"Okay, kid. I'll take you to William and have him encode the elevator with your thumbprint. However, I'll have you wear a locator cuff. And just to make things clear, the thing is impossible to remove by anyone but William. Not without cutting off your hand. Still want one?"

"Hell, yeah! Sure I want it! It's not like I have any desire to leave or anything. " Michael shook Kian's hand vigorously. "Thank you. I hate being locked up."

"You're welcome."

"How about me? Don't I get a thumbprint pass to the elevator?" Syssi hadn't thought to ask before, but now with Michael getting it, she saw no reason why she shouldn't have access to the elevators as well.

"You don't have one yet? I thought Amanda took care of it. How did you get around?"

"There was always someone escorting me. I never used the elevator by myself. Frankly, at one point I even considered taking the endless stairs down. I'm getting claustrophobic being cooped up in here."

"Both of you are coming with me to William right now to take care of this." Kian led them toward another turn in the endless labyrinth of the underground.

"If I'm to navigate it on my own, I'll need a map of this place. Otherwise, I'll get so lost, it will take you days to find me." Syssi wasn't joking. Besides the place being huge, there were no distinguishing signs between one corridor and another. They all looked the same; same industrial carpet, same concrete walls, and the same metal doors leading to various rooms. With her nonexistent sense of direction, she would be lost in no time.

A wicked gleam in his eyes, Kian bent to whisper in her ear. "I'll slap a locator cuff on you as well, my sweet."

"Aren't you the big bad wolf." She stretched up on her tiptoes, pretending to go for his lips. But instead of the kiss he'd been expecting, she nipped his nose.

"Oh, I'll get you for that…" Kian growled.

"As I see it, I owed you a bite… or two… you had it coming…"

"You're lucky we have company…" Kian pinched her butt.

Michael chuckled.

"Shut up, kid. You haven't seen a thing…" He twisted back, pinning Michael with a hard stare.

"I see nothing, hear nothing… I'm not even here…" Michael saluted solemnly, his face pinched in an effort to suppress another chuckle.

"You and I are going to get along just fine, kid…" Kian winked at Michael, then wrapped his arm around Syssi's waist, pulling her closer against his side.

3

SYSSI

*B*ack at the penthouse, Syssi examined the wide metal cuff on her wrist. It didn't look too bad. The highly polished metal gleamed like a fine piece of jewelry, and the cuff's unbreakable locking mechanism was so cleverly concealed that no one would ever suspect the thing housed a sophisticated tracking device.

Except, regrettably, the pretty cuff would trigger an alarm as soon as she tried to leave the compound.

And here she thought she would be free to roam the streets whenever she pleased.

With that thought, Syssi slanted a suspicious glance at Kian, who was sitting beside her on the couch, busy going through his emails on an iPad. "How come you have these cuffs in the first place?"

Lifting his head, he deposited the device on the coffee table and leaned toward her. "For house arrests. If a clan member broke one of our laws, he or she might be sentenced to house arrest or, in the case of restriction, allowed to leave only for school or work. The cuff ensures compliance with sentencing."

"Interesting. It didn't occur to me that you need to govern yourselves separately from the mortal population. Although it makes sense. With your special abilities, someone needs to keep things in check, right? So is it like a monarchy or a democracy? And who makes the laws? Who enforces them? And who is the judge?"

Pausing to take a breath, she smiled apologetically at Kian's amused expression. "I'm sorry for blasting you with so many questions, but this is so fascinating. Oh, and how are your laws different from ours?"

"Our laws are not that different. The two clan specific issues are keeping our existence secret and the use of thralls and illusions. The teenagers are the most difficult to control. Imagine being able to thrall the bartender to sell you a drink, your teacher to raise your grades, or the pretty girl in your math class to get intimate with you. Even good kids might be tempted. And as in any society, we have our share of bad apples. The adults are less problematic. Not because they are all well-behaved angels, but because they are better aware of the consequences." Kian shrugged.

"We maintain a small police force, the Guardians, all of whom you've already met. Arrests are made and the perpetrators are brought before a judge or a panel of judges, depending on the severity of their crime. For the most severe cases, the whole clan has to vote. Sentencing varies from monetary fines to house arrests to incarceration here in the underground, etc."

Syssi was impressed. "Wow! You guys are like a country within a country. With your own laws, police force, judges, jails... So, do you get a lot of unlawful behavior?"

"Not a lot, but enough, mostly minor infractions. If you're really interested, I can arrange for you to meet Edna. She is our legal expert, attorney, judge... Everything you want to know regarding clan law, she'll be more than happy to tell you all about it in excruciating detail. She loves the law, and she loves talking about it even more. But what I want you to do now is come with me to the kitchen and eat something. You look pale."

"I'm a little hungry... come to think of it, I didn't have lunch yet." Syssi followed Kian to the kitchen and took a seat at the counter, not sure if she should offer to make something or let him play host.

"Let's see..." Kian poked his head into the refrigerator. "No worries, Okidu left us lunch." He pulled out a container of pasta and a large bowl of salad. After warming the pasta in the microwave for a few minutes, he brought both over to the counter.

"By the way, where is Okidu? I'm surprised he is not here to fuss around us like we're a couple of helpless children who need to be fed."

"Probably went grocery shopping." Kian stuffed a large swirl of pasta into his mouth.

"You're so lucky to have him. He is an outstanding cook, everything he makes is delicious." Syssi ate slowly, taking small bites to savor the taste.

"Yeah, he is great... Though speaking of delicious food... I was wondering if you'd like to go out with me to a restaurant tomorrow night. If you think Okidu's is good, the food there will blow away your taste buds. I thought dinner and some dancing would be nice. What do you say?"

"That sounds wonderful." *He is actually taking me out on a date!* A spark of hope shimmered in her heart. "I'd love to go out with you." *A romantic outing...* "But just to a restaurant, not to a club. I don't like the scene. Last night, I was very uncomfortable. I'm not in the mood to repeat that experience anytime soon."

"No, not a club, I don't like them either." Kian twisted toward her and swiveled her stool, bracketing her knees between his thighs so they were facing each other. "The restaurant I'm talking about has live music and dancing. It's not loud, and the clientele is very exclusive. Just to get in you need to be a member, or be invited by one. It's a bit snobby, but the upside of that is an atmosphere that is posh and romantic, not vulgar like the club's. I guarantee you're going to love it."

"What is it called?"

"*By Invitation Only.*"

"Seriously? That's the name? It's like naming your dog, Dog." She snorted. It wasn't really that funny, but she was giddy. *I'm such a fool, it's only a date.* "I've never heard of it."

"Of course not. Those who are willing to spend that kind of money on a membership do so as much for the privacy as for the exclusivity. It would defeat the whole purpose of the place if the paparazzi got a whiff of it and descended on it like a pack of hounds, hunting for the celebrities."

"You've got a point... So, should I assume you're a member? Or did you pull some strings to get us invited?"

"I'm part owner of the place. After graduating from the culinary institute, a nephew of mine came asking if I would be willing to loan him the money he needed to open his own place. I liked the concept, not to mention the taste of what he had prepared for me to try. So, I made it an investment instead of a loan. He runs it, and I collect a share of the profits. Win-win for both of us."

"Is everyone in your family a member?"

"Definitely not, just the ones we invite and who are willing to pay for membership…"

"What about those you don't invite? They must feel left out."

"What they don't know won't hurt them. Anyway, the place was not intended to be a family hangout. The concept was to provide a top-notch place for the rich and famous—the movers and shakers of society—to mingle and have fun away from the public eye."

"And you want to take plain old me to hang out with those kinds of people? I'll stick out like a sore thumb. What will I wear? I don't know how to dress for a place like this." She cringed, some of her initial excitement ebbing. "Can't we go somewhere less intimidating?" As much as she was intrigued, she couldn't help thinking of how awkward she'd feel amongst such a crowd.

"Nonsense, Amanda will take you shopping and get you everything you need. You know it's her favorite pastime… Well, maybe second favorite… Anyway, just leave it to her and you'll be fine; she is a pro when it comes to fashion. And besides, you need to get out of here and get some fresh air, even if it's the somewhat polluted type that hangs over Rodeo Drive. I'm certain you'll have fun on an outing with her."

Syssi was sure she would, but the idea of spending a small fortune just so she could fit in with the patrons of a snooty place for one night didn't sit well with her pragmatic nature. And shopping at a place like Rodeo Drive? Not going to happen.

Maybe I could borrow something from Amanda—that makes much more sense.

"Okay, I'll go… Just for once, I'm curious to see how the elite parties. But I'm not sure about buying new expensive stuff that I'll probably never wear again."

"Don't worry about the money—it's my treat."

"I have the money. I just hate spending it frivolously."

"Please, do it for me. I feel so bad for turning your life upside down.

Getting you something you would never buy for yourself will bring me much pleasure. Be a good girl and say yes."

"I'll think about it. First, I'm going to see if I can borrow something from Amanda." It was hard to say no to him, but she didn't want to accept presents from Kian just so he could ease his conscience. This was exactly what her parents had done every time they had neglected her or her siblings. They had bought expensive presents; after a long absence, or for not showing up for teacher conferences, or school plays, or sports games, or graduations… It had been nothing but a bribe.

"There is nothing to think about. If I'm dragging you to this expensive place, I think I should be the one to provide you with whatever you need to feel comfortable going there. Case closed." Kian really wasn't used to anyone saying no to him, and with the way his brows were tightening, Syssi realized he was getting impatient with her.

"My big bad wolf… You can huff, and you can puff, but this little piggy will not bow down." She leaned to nip at his nose again.

"We'll see about that…" On a surge, he gripped her at the waist and pulled her up, then tossed her over his shoulder. With his arm locked over her thighs, he strode down the hallway toward his bedroom, playfully smacking her upturned behind.

"Put me down, you brute!" Laughing, Syssi pounded her fists on his back.

"Oh, I will… as soon as we reach the bed. Then I'll put you down… over my knee to finish what I've started." He delivered a stronger smack that actually managed to sting a little.

"Oh, no you will not. Put me down this instant!" Giggling hysterically and fighting to catch her breath, she was barely able to get the words out. But secretly, she was incredibly turned on and wondered how far Kian would take this game… Or more to the point… how far she wanted him to take it…

4

KIAN

K ian smiled smugly as he inhaled the intoxicating aroma of Syssi's arousal. The minx was turned on by the little scene he was enacting, and he wondered how far she would like to be pushed.

The truth was that even though his predatory nature attracted those with spicier tastes, he had never had the urge to test his partners' limits before. And during the short interludes he was accustomed to, he mostly followed their cues.

Except, that was with women he hadn't been emotionally invested in and hadn't really cared how they had felt about him. It was different with Syssi. With her, he had an overbearing craving to push the envelope and see how far she was willing to go.

On some level it disturbed him; he wished he didn't have these kinds of urges. But given the predatory nature of his people, there wasn't much he could do about it. Fuck knew, most of the males of his kind were beasts, and even the females were rapacious. Only those further away from the source seemed to get their genetically preprogrammed impulses somewhat diluted.

In his case, however, he was as close to the source as it got.

Being dominant and aggressive had been an advantage in the era he had been born into; as a natural leader and fighter he had what it took to safeguard his family. But as times had changed, and what had been required of him had shifted toward the diplomatic and managerial, he had learned to keep these impulses on a tight leash.

It was a constant struggle.

Growing up without a father, or any other male of his kind to look up to and emulate, he had chosen as his role models the few mortal men that over the years had gained his respect. And the type of man he admired and believed he ought to be wasn't the fierce warrior or the ruthless commander.

It was the cultured gentleman: polite, lenient and accommodating.

Civilized.

Except, with Syssi it seemed his civilized facade was cracking—the fissures getting wider—and last night, in that damned elevator, the false veneer had shattered completely.

That being said, he was all too aware that Syssi liked this side of him—at least to some degree. But the thing that gave him pause, the reason he strained to rein in the beast, was that he might cross the line and scare her off.

He wanted to bring her nothing but pleasure; to be the one and only to fulfill all of her wildest desires. And by doing so, some of his own.

Sitting down on the bed, he lowered her down over his knees, just as he had promised. And as he caressed her denim-clad bottom, his other palm resting between her shoulder blades and holding her down gently, he waited to see if she'd try to get free.

She didn't. Turning her head sideways, Syssi laid her cheek on the comforter, holding her breath in strained anticipation.

"You know it's only a game? That I would never hurt you?" he asked quietly, his voice raspy with his arousal.

"Yes," she answered, her throaty whisper betraying how much she wanted this.

5

SYSSI

hy? Syssi had no clue. She had never done anything like that before. Hell, she had never even thought about it. Up until she had met Kian, she had been convinced she was purely vanilla: and a very boring flavor of vanilla at that. What could be so damn arousing about a spanking?

Something must be really wrong with her to be so turned on by the prospect of what she should find at least degrading, if not scary and completely wrong.

On some level, she hoped she would hate it—that it would hurt and prove to be a big turnoff—because that would make her normal.

Not kinky and weird.

As Kian yanked down her jeans with her panties coming along for the ride, she bit down on her lower lip, and feeling the cool air on her exposed bottom, fought the urge to giggle and make him stop. But she forced herself to stay put. Resolved to find out once and for all what it was like. To have the experience so she could put that demon to rest—one way or the other.

With his hand lightly caressing her bottom, Kian inhaled sharply through his clenched teeth, making the kind of hissing sound that she came to expect before his bite. Syssi tensed, bracing for his fangs. Instead, she felt his soft lips, kissing each cheek before he went back to caressing them.

"You have a gorgeous ass, Syssi, small and perfectly plump…," he said with that same snakelike hiss as his finger stroked over her drenched folds. "And you're soaking wet… my sweet girl."

Syssi groaned. Then she almost climaxed when he brushed lightly over her sensitive, throbbing bundle of nerves.

Between her fearful anticipation and his light caresses, Syssi was so turned on she felt like crawling out of her skin. "Please…" she pleaded, not knowing what exactly she was pleading for. At this point, she would've done just about anything to get what she needed to hurtle over that strained edge.

Answering her plea, Kian's palm descended, landing with a light smack on her upturned behind. But it was not enough, she needed more. The next three landed in quick succession, but he was still being too gentle with her, and she was getting antsy. Pushing her bottom up with a little wiggle, she tried to communicate her need for him to do better without having to say a thing.

"Greedy little minx, aren't you?" He smacked her bottom harder, finally bringing on the sting she craved. After five more delicious smacks, the small ache pulsing in her behind was almost enough to send her over the precipice. She groaned again, waiting. But he stopped.

"Not yet, sweet girl, I want to be inside you when you come," he growled. With a quick surge, he moved her over, pulling up her hips so she was propped on her knees with her cheek still pressed down to the mattress.

While caressing her warmed-up bottom with his palm, Kian struggled to pull down his pants with the other. He ended up only pushing them down past his hips, and with a grunt, thrust inside her from behind.

Syssi felt as if a tight rubber band had snapped, and as she was flung over that cliff, she flew apart. Kian kept his hold on her hips, preventing her from being shoved forward as he kept pounding into her and prolonging her climax.

As his pelvis kept slapping against her tender behind, the explosive combination of the submissive pose and his forceful thrusts had her orgasm two more times. Though coming one on the heel of the other, they felt like one long rapture crashing to shore in several powerful waves.

Drained to the point of passing out, Syssi thought she couldn't take it anymore. Except, Kian wasn't done yet. Pulling on her hair, he brought her up so she was kneeling with her back pressed against his chest. His arm holding her in an iron grip around her middle, he tilted her head and with a loud hiss sank his fangs into her exposed neck.

Syssi found she still had some hidden reserves, climaxing again when Kian's venom and his seed flooded her body.

With a keening moan that sounded more like a weak sob escaping her dry, hoarse throat, she collapsed—utterly drained yet completely sated.

6

KIAN

With Syssi still cradled in his arms, Kian plopped down on his side and smirked.

At this rate, they were going to drain each other dry until there was nothing left of them but two shriveled husks.

Oh, but what a way to go.

Feeling oddly at peace, he stroked Syssi's damp hair and wrapped himself tighter against her back, letting sleep slowly claim him...

Kian found himself in the small, one-room house he had shared with his wife all those centuries ago. He snuggled closer to the woman sleeping in his arms, dimly aware that he was dreaming and that the warm body he was spooning didn't belong to Lavena.

Rubbing his erection against her naked bottom, he buried his nose in her hair. "Hmm... You smell so good, love," he whispered in her ear before nuzzling her neck.

She turned in his arms, lifting her sweet lips for a kiss. "Good morning, my love."

"Morning?" The rooster crowed outside. "Good morning it is, then." He took her mouth, his tongue parting her lips.

She pulled away. "No French-kissing—morning breath."

"I don't care." He pulled her back and covered her with his body, pinning

29

her to the bed. Catching both of her wrists in one hand, he stretched her arms over her head.

Her body went soft, surrendering, and she closed her eyes. Kian took his time exploring her mouth at leisure. Syssi parted her legs, cradling him.

"I love you," he whispered in her ear as he sank into her wet heat.

"Don't leave me..." she whispered back, a tear sliding down her rosy cheek.

"Why would I ever leave you? I love you. You know it, right?" He looked into her sad eyes.

How could she ask him that? Why on earth would he leave her?

Everything was perfect. He was making love to his beautiful woman in the home they'd built together.

What more could a man want?

7

SYSSI

With Kian's warm body enveloping her from behind, and his heavy arm draped over her middle—palm resting splayed-fingered against her belly—Syssi felt a delightful, inner quiet.

She opened her eyes. It couldn't have been long since she'd passed out because the sun, shining brightly through the glass walls of the terrace doors, was still pretty high in the sky.

They were both a mess; still dressed, their pants bunched around their ankles, and Kian's groin was sticking wetly to her behind.

Evidently, he had been too wiped out to perform his cleaning routine. Funny, how this little thing made him seem more human to her—proving that he wasn't Superman after all.

Although in her humble opinion, he came pretty damn close.

Smiling contentedly, she lifted his hand to her lips and kissed the inside of his palm, then rubbed it against her cheek.

I love this man. She sighed.

There was no point in denying it. She didn't want to fall in love with him, knew it was going to break her heart, but to keep pretending wasn't doing her any good either.

She'd be deceiving no one but herself.

Oh, God, she felt like crying.

31

But if she cried now, it would be as good as admitting that there was no hope, nothing she could do, and Syssi wasn't ready to throw in the towel yet.

Accepting defeat without a fight wasn't something she was capable of— even over a losing battle like her relationship with Gregg. She should've ended it long before it had fizzled and died on its own. But not willing to admit failure, she had kept fighting for it when it would've been smarter to let him go.

It wasn't the same, though. In this case, the end was beyond her control. But what she did in the interim wasn't. Pulling her resolve around her like a suit of armor, she made up her mind to be grateful for whatever she could have with Kian and not succumb to despair over what was not to be.

Still, it was easier said than done.

With another sigh, she gently extracted herself from Kian's embrace. After wiggling out of her pants, she tiptoed bare-assed to the bathroom, washed up, then soaked some washcloths in warm water for Kian.

Sleeping like a dead man, he didn't stir as she wiped the sticky residue from his groin. Though true to form, her ministrations got him instantly hard.

Yep, Superman indeed. Syssi chuckled.

After tossing the washcloths in the laundry bin, she returned to the bed and snuggled back into Kian's arms.

His striking face was peaceful in sleep, and she realized that when awake, he had always looked strained. *Poor baby, shouldering the weight of the world, literally.*

Stroking his cheek, she felt her heart overflow with love and, unexpectedly, a sense of gratitude. It was a strange emotion to have after the bit of naughty they'd played. And yet, it was how she felt. Grateful for the incredible pleasure—for the freedom to experience things with him without the fear of ridicule or rejection.

In the few days they had known each other, he'd never criticized her, had never implied she was anything less than perfect in his eyes.

Kian accepted all of her the way she was. Even her little kink...

Syssi smiled as the gleam from her cuff caught her eye. Kian was pretty kinky himself. The obvious thrill he had gotten from locking the thing on her wrist gave her an inkling to his own twisted desires. She'd have to pry them out of him—curious to see what tickled his fancy.

Confident in the reassuring safety of his care... or was it his love? She was willing to try new things.

Except, how long did she have?

Closing her eyes, she tried to hold back the tears, but her imaginary coat of armor was crumbling under the onslaught of the dark shadows cast by the reality of their situation.

If she still believed in a benevolent God, she would have prayed reverently for a fairy-tale ending to their story; her turning immortal, the two of them spending eternity together... raising children...

The whole happily-ever-after thing.

But after her brother's death, she had lost her faith in happy endings. If there was a real deity somewhere, it didn't listen to prayers or care about the individual parts of the multitudes of its creation.

Chaos ruled, and bad things happened to good people all the time. At any moment, all of this could be taken away from her, without even the memories to sustain her.

Then again, maybe it was a blessing in disguise.

If she didn't remember any of it, she wouldn't have to live with the pain of losing it. Except, what was worse? Never to know what she was privileged to experience, or to remember and mourn its loss?

Feeling Kian's gentle finger wipe away the traitorous tear caught in her lashes, her lids fluttered open.

"What's the matter, baby?" he asked, then kissed her eyelids. "Was it too much? I thought you liked it..." He frowned, looking apprehensive.

"No, it's not that. I did like it..." Embarrassed, she felt her face heat up. "It's just that I don't want us to end..." she whispered, and a few more tears escaped despite her valiant effort to hold them back.

"We will not..." Kian pulled her tightly against his chest. "If you don't turn, I'll just chain you naked to my bed and keep you as my sex slave forever." He kissed her forehead, stroking her back in small soothing circles.

She chuckled. "You'd like that, wouldn't you?"

"We'll figure something out. I don't think I could let you go, no matter what." He sighed and bent his head to kiss her lips.

"Even if I stay on as your sex slave..." Syssi smiled a sad little smile. "The cold reality is that I'll grow old while you won't. And that's the biggest obstacle in this wishful fantasy. As much as I hate to admit it, you were right. If I don't turn, you'll have to let me go."

His eyes were so sad, she knew she was going to flay him with what she was compelled to say next. "I just wish you could leave me my memories, so I could relive our time together in my mind and know that I lived to experience something wonderful and treasure it forever... despite how torturous knowing I had this and lost it will surely be."

"Oh, baby." He choked as he held her close—his pain echoing hers. "All we can do is hope. I know hope is for fools and children, but I have nothing else."

"I know... neither do I." She kissed his chest through his T-shirt, a few more tears wetting the soft fabric. And yet, there was comfort to be had in the knowledge that he was just as pained by their dim prospects as she was. Which in turn, as absurd as the notion was, made her want to be strong enough for both of them.

The irony, of an almost twenty-five-year-old mortal thinking she could shore up an almost two-thousand-year-old superbeing, wasn't lost on her. Nevertheless, she went on to imagine her armor snapping back into place— this time extending over Kian as well.

With a big brave smile plastered on her face, she kissed his warm lips. "Well, I for one am done moping around. There is no point in lamenting that which cannot be changed. We just have to take it one day at a time. Right?" She glanced down at her watch. "Anyway, I need to get back to work, it's late."

"What time is it?" Kian asked.

"It's ten past four."

"Oh, damn, I have a meeting scheduled for four-thirty."

"I need to go too. Amanda must be wondering why I'm not back yet." Syssi scooted off the bed and grabbed her pants off the floor, then pulled them on. "Ugh, yak! My panties are wet!" She pulled them back down. "Can I borrow a pair of yours? I hate wearing jeans with no underwear. Too rough on my sensitive girl parts..." She waggled her brows.

"Sure, I'll trade you a clean pair of mine for yours." His tone promised something wicked was to follow. "I'm going to carry your sweet-smelling panties in my pocket, and whenever I miss you, I'll take sniffs of your essence."

Syssi laughed. "You're a pervert, you know that? Catch!" She threw her panties at his face.

"Ah, Syssi…" Kian caught the little scrap of satin and lace and crushed it to his nose, taking a loud sniff. "Delicious…" He sniffed again, taunting her while she ran into his closet to get a pair of his boxer briefs.

"You should really get your stuff back in here. It's kind of pointless to leave it at Amanda's when you keep ending up here anyway." He stuffed her panties in his back pocket.

"I will. Now give me back my undies, I need to put them in the wash." She extended her arm.

"Ah, ah, ah… a deal is a deal. I'm keeping them." He pulled her in for a scorching kiss.

Coming up for air, she said, "I thought you needed to be somewhere…"

"Yeah, how unfortunate…" He let her pull out from his arms. "You'll be at Amanda's?"

"Yes, and if you miss me, you can call me on this brand-new, wonderful phone I got instead of sniffing my panties…" Syssi pulled the device out of her pocket, caressing its sleek surface. "Precious…," she whispered coarsely like Sméagol from *Lord of the Rings.*

"Let's go, Sméagol." Kian tousled her hair. Outside Amanda's door, he kissed her hard before letting her go. "I'll see you later."

8

SYSSI

"*L*ucy! I'm home!" Syssi called as she opened the door.

Rushing out of the kitchen and waving her hands in a damn good imitation of the legendary Lucy, Amanda chirped, "Oh, Ricky, darling!"

The woman was a born actress.

"Sorry I took so long, I'll get to work right away."

"Rubbish, it's not important. Come, talk to me. Tell me what you've been up to. You should have been done with Bridget hours ago." Amanda dragged her by the hand to sit beside her on the couch. "I see that Kian cuffed you." She lifted Syssi's forearm to examine the cuff.

"Yeah, I have access to the elevators now, and so does Michael. Now both of us can spy on you guys and uncover all of your dirty little secrets."

"Very funny… So, what else have you been up to, besides having your blood drawn and getting… cuffed…"

"Kian asked me out on a date for tomorrow night. He wants to take me to this very posh restaurant…" Syssi was pretty sure Amanda was a member, but just in case, she skirted around the name of the place.

"He's taking you to *By Invitation Only*? That's wonderful!" Amanda squeezed Syssi in her arms as if she had just delivered the best of news.

"That's the one… but why are you so excited?"

36

"How could I not be? It's the first time that I know of, that is, Kian has asked anyone on a date! I'm going to have to drink to that. Margarita?" She walked up to the bar.

"Yeah, why not, bring it on…" A drink actually sounded wonderful.

"How is it possible he has never done that before? What about all the women he's shagged?"

"You've seen me in action. Would you call what I do dating?" Amanda handed her the drink and took a sip of her own.

"No, I guess not… So that's all you guys do? Pick up random strangers for hookups?"

"Yep, told you it sucks… The sex is okay, though, most of the time…" Amanda grimaced.

"I couldn't live that way. Now I understand what Kian meant when he said he hated it." Syssi took a big sip of the cold drink.

"Hey, we need to go shopping!" Amanda's eyes lit up with excitement. "I'm thinking a whole morning of girl fun. We'll go for a facial. A manicure and pedicure are an absolute must, then the hair salon complete with professional makeup. And then… Ta-Da! Rodeo Drive!"

"I can't afford all that!" Syssi laughed at Amanda's enthusiasm.

Dismissing Syssi's monetary concerns, Amanda waved her hand. "Don't be silly. I'm going to charge it all to Kian's card."

"You can't do that! I don't want him spending a small fortune on clothes I'll use for only one night. Where will I wear stuff like this? Starbucks?"

"He doesn't care about the money. You know he can afford it. But he cares about you, and you're not going to be selfish and refuse. You're going to let him do this small thing for you, just to make him happy. *Capisce?*" Amanda arched her well-defined dark brow and took another sip from her drink.

That shut Syssi up, effectively making any further arguments seem petty. She realized Amanda was right. Kian had made it clear that it would please him to pamper her.

So why was she still making waves about it?

Was it pride?

To some extent… But mostly it was about who she was and what she believed in. Spending obscene amounts on clothes or shoes seemed vain and frivolous to her. Still, she had to consider that what seemed obscene to her was perfectly reasonable to Kian and Amanda. And if she wanted to hang out with them at places like that fancy restaurant, she had to fit in with the rest of their rich friends.

"Okay, you win...," she conceded.

"Yay! I'm so happy!" Amanda hugged her again. "We're going to have so much fun."

"You're going to have fun. I, on the other hand, am not such a big fan of beauty salons and shopping. I lose patience real quick."

"Don't worry. With me by your side... there won't be a dull moment."

"Oh, I'm sure you're right... there is never a dull moment when you're around." Feeling the margarita's effect, Syssi laughed. "That's what I'll miss going back to Kian's... He asked me to bring my stuff back to his place."

"You do that, as you never actually sleep here... But no worries; we'll have plenty of good times together. It's not like I'm a long commute away, right?"

"Right... Well, I'm going to pack my stuff and then finally do some work." Syssi walked over to the kitchen to rinse out her glass.

"Okay, party pooper. Now you've guilted me into doing some work as well." Amanda pushed up from the couch and sauntered over to the bar. Making herself another drink, she turned to Syssi. "Want one?" she asked.

"No, thank you, I don't want a repeat of what happened the last time you kept pushing margaritas at me..." Syssi grimaced and headed for her room to pack.

It didn't take long until most of her belongings were neatly folded and packed into the duffle bag. But when she got to the velvet pouch containing her modest collection of jewelry, instead of adding it to the rest of her stuff, she turned around and dumped its contents on top of the dresser.

Sifting through the small pile of earrings, she sighed. None would work for her date with Kian. The diamond studs were okay, but they were as good as invisible beneath her full, wavy hair, and the rest of the stuff was just too plain for the occasion.

The same was true for the necklaces and bracelets. None of the bracelets would look good matched with the gleaming silver cuff on her right hand. And as for the necklaces, she didn't feel like taking off Andrew's pendant for something flashier even if the gold didn't go with the silver of the cuff.

"Oh, well…" Syssi returned everything to the pouch. Turning around, she found Amanda leaning against the doorjamb and sipping from her drink.

"I'll be right back," Amanda said. Leaving her goblet on the dresser, she stepped out and headed down the hallway.

A few minutes later, she returned with an ornate jewelry box. Placing it on the dresser, she lifted its lid with marked reverence.

Inside, nestled in black velvet, was a gorgeous set of platinum and diamond earrings and a matching necklace. Syssi had never seen jewelry as beautiful as this. And even though she knew next to nothing about the styles or designer names of the fine-jewelry world, she had no doubt it was a one of a kind masterpiece.

"I want you to wear this tomorrow." Amanda put her hand on Syssi's shoulder. "Go ahead… try it on…," she urged.

"Are you serious? Would you really let me borrow this for tomorrow? It's stunning! Where did you get it? It must be one of a kind."

"It is. It was a present from my mother for my two-hundredth birthday. I have no idea who she commissioned to make it, but I'm certain she ensured it was the only one made." Amanda ran her fingers over the surface of the beautiful necklace.

"It must be very special to you. I will feel weird wearing it… even for one evening." As much as Syssi was tempted, she knew she would be constantly stressed and worried that something might happen to it. The set was price-less, irreplaceable.

"You mean a lot to me, Syssi." Amanda's tone got so uncharacteristically serious, it compelled Syssi to pry her gaze away from the jewelry and look up at her friend's face.

Amanda still wore that reverent expression, except, it wasn't directed at the masterpiece in the box. She was looking at Syssi.

Syssi's eyes misted with emotion. "You mean a lot to me too." She wrapped her arm around Amanda's shoulders and pulled her into a hug.

Amanda leaned into her for a moment, her soft hair brushing against Syssi's neck. Then pulling back, she placed both hands on Syssi's shoulders and pinned her with her intense blue stare. "In the short time I've known you, I've come to think of you as a sister. I'm not that close to my real sisters, who are much older and busy with their own responsibilities, and I only became close to Kian when I moved here and he took me under his wing. But regardless of how things will turn out for the two of you, my feelings for you will not change. I want you to have the set, not only for tomorrow but to keep—as a symbol of our friendship."

Touching a finger to Syssi's lips, Amanda shushed her protests. "Hear me out. I want to give you something that has a special meaning to me and is close to my heart. And I can't think of anything else that will better fit the bill. Money means nothing to me, so anything I may buy for you wouldn't be special enough. Don't say no, let me have the pleasure of knowing you are carrying on your person a token of my love."

Syssi was moved to tears. At some point during the last several days, she'd grown to care deeply for the complicated woman; there was no way she was going to jeopardize their nascent bond by being callous with Amanda's feelings. And as she saw no way to refuse without offending her friend, she was left with no choice but to accept.

But she'd have to gift Amanda something of equal value back. Except, the value would have to be in the sentiment it carried since she didn't own anything even remotely close to the monetary worth of that set. Syssi suspected that even her car, which had been pretty expensive, wasn't worth that much.

This left only one thing she could think of. Grasping at the necklace Andrew had given her on her sixteenth birthday, she opened the tiny clasp and took it off.

"If I'm to accept this gift from you, then you have to accept this from me. This necklace was a gift from my brother Andrew, and since the day I got it I never left home without it. It's not nearly as valuable as what you gave me, but if you believe objects get imbued with their owner's essence, then this necklace has the most essence I have ever imparted on any one thing. I regret the fact that it isn't worth even a fraction of what your gift is. My only consolation is that when you wear it, you'll carry some of me with you." She took Amanda's hand and pressed the delicate chain with its small heart pendant into her palm.

"Thank you. I'm going to wear it always, just the way you did…" Amanda wrapped the chain around her neck and closed the clasp. When she was done adjusting the diamond-encrusted heart to lie in the hollow of her neck, she swiped a finger under each of her teary eyes. "Come here…" She opened her arms, inviting Syssi to step into another embrace.

Standing in each other's arms, they were both sniffling. It felt good, though, to acknowledge this bond between them.

Syssi wondered what was it that had brought them so close together in such a short time. Was it the love they shared for Kian? Or was it the fact that they were both survivors of similar tragedies?

Or maybe it was the attraction of opposites?

On the surface of things, they had nothing in common; different looks, different temperaments, different values. They didn't even belong to the same species for goodness' sake. Except, it seemed like they were both in desperate need of a good friend.

9

ANDREW

eady to be done for the day, Andrew closed the Maldives case file when his phone rang.

He frowned. An unknown caller? No one besides a select few that were already on his contacts list was supposed to have this number. On an impulse, he accepted the call instead of letting it go to voice mail. "Yes?" he barked.

"Is it a bad time? You sound busy."

"Syssi, I thought you were a wrong number... No, not busy at all, what's up?"

As it was, Andrew still had no new leads on that damned case. He had searched everything he could think of; going through the registration records of every hotel, motel, and inn he had access to. Which, unless they were not connected to the internet, meant everything with rooms for rent in the greater Los Angeles area. He had even gone as far as checking every group of four men or more registering at the same time, and when that had produced zilch, he'd narrowed it down to three.

The twelve had disappeared without a trace. If they were still somewhere around LA, they were most likely staying at someone's private residence. Unless they got themselves into some kind of trouble, he would have no way of locating them.

"Just wanted to give you my new cell phone number and tell you that I'm still at Amanda's, working on that report."

"I thought you were calling from a blocked landline. Why didn't you keep your old cell number?" Andrew's bullshit radar switched on, its red alert light blinking like crazy. "What aren't you telling me, Syssi?"

The sigh she'd heaved had him jack upright in his chair and tighten his grip on the phone. What kind of trouble had she gotten herself into?

"I didn't want to worry you... but Amanda's lab was ransacked a couple of nights ago. That's why we are working at her place instead of the lab."

"We'll get to why you didn't tell me about this before, after you explain what the hell this has to do with you changing your phone number." Pushing up from his chair, Andrew began pacing around.

When instead of providing an explanation she sighed again, he felt like punching someone. Except, with no ready candidates lined up, he ended up smashing his fist into the concrete wall and bruising his knuckles instead. "Talk!" he grated. If she sighed one more time, he was driving over there and shaking the truth out of her.

Did she think to coddle him?

"It was a hate crime. A group of religious fanatics that think Amanda's research has some occult ramifications. They stole a list of her test subjects —the ones with paranormal abilities. I was at the top of that list, and Amanda was afraid they'd come after me, as well as one of the other high ranked talents. That's why both of us are staying at her family's place. I had to get rid of my phone so they will have no way of tracking me..."

"And it didn't cross your mind to call me? Who's better equipped to protect you? Amanda or me? I can't believe you acted so irresponsibly. And what are the police doing about it?" Striding back to his desk, Andrew sat down and booted up his terminal.

"The police are investigating, but they think it's just a malicious prank. And I didn't come to you because there was no need. Amanda's place is in a highly secure building, as in Fort Knox secure. You have nothing to worry about. And besides, if I stayed with you, I wouldn't be able to continue my work with her, and as you are well aware, I do need to work for a living." Syssi huffed as if to say, "You see? I was completely reasonable."

"Even so, you could have let me know. You know the resources available to me…"

"I know, I'm sorry. But really, there is no need for you to get involved in this. I'm sure the whole thing will blow over in a few days."

"I'll look into it and see what I can do. Bummer, though…"

"Yeah, I know. There are some crazy loons out there."

"That too, but that's not what I'm bummed about. I was hoping you were shacking up with a guy and covering it up… It's about time you got something going on."

10

SYSSI

Syssi took a fortifying breath before plunging headfirst into the deep. "Amanda does have a brother…"

"I knew it!" Andrew chuckled before switching into his interrogator mode. "And how is that brother of hers?"

"He is fine, like in *really* fine. But there's nothing for you to get all worked up about. There is not much to tell." Syssi cringed. *If lightning indeed struck liars, I would be a smoking husk right now.*

"I want to meet him." Andrew got that resolute tone that meant he wouldn't take no for an answer.

"I just met him, for God's sake. Perfect way to scare the guy off… Oh, by the way, my big brother wants to give you the third degree… Really, it's nothing to worry about, just an interrogation from hell—the kind reserved for suspected terrorists and serial killers… Not going to happen, Andrew. I don't want it to be over before it even begins."

I'd better step aside to avoid that lightning when it strikes me where I stand…

"Okay, okay… You've got a point…," he conceded. "So, how about you introduce me to this Amanda I keep hearing about? I can question her instead… You were nagging me to meet her anyway, true?"

He got her there. Now she couldn't refuse.

"I can arrange something with Amanda, but no questions! And I mean it!

45

You're not going to embarrass me in front of my boss who happens also to be my best friend." Syssi was surprised by her own words. It was true, though, and a warmth spread through her at the realization.

"I'm glad you are BFFs with your boss. I promise I'll be discreet. You can kick me in the shin if I cross the line."

As if summoned by being the subject of their conversation, Amanda walked in. "Who are you talking to?" she asked.

"It's Andrew. He wants to meet you..."

"I would love to meet your fascinating brother." Amanda sat down next to Syssi and opened her laptop. "How about lunch, tomorrow, after our shopping spree? There is this great little Italian café not far from Rodeo, Café Milano. Ask him if he can meet us there at around three."

"Did I hear right? Shopping on Rodeo Drive? You never even pay retail, let alone visit high-end boutiques." Andrew sounded amused.

"I know... don't ask..." Syssi snorted.

"Tomorrow at three, Café Milano, tell your boss I'll be there."

"See you there." Syssi ended the call and shook her head at Amanda.

Typing away on her laptop, the distinguished professor, Dr. Amanda Dokani, was quietly singing, "Bad boy, bad boy, whatcha gonna do, whatcha gonna do when Amanda comes for you..."

11

KIAN

On his way to the meeting, Kian reflected on the fact that although he had never resented his work before, he did now. Damn, he would've loved to stay in bed with Syssi and cuddle, or maybe go for another round... But then, she had work to do as well.

Fuck that.

He should've just told her to stay.

If it were up to him, he'd make sure that unless Syssi wanted to, she wouldn't have to work another day in her life. Though, knowing Syssi, she would not have liked him managing her like that, and besides, she seemed to love her work.

Kian sighed. This whole train of thought was pointless. Even if he could persuade Syssi to slack, there was no escaping his responsibilities, and the Guardians he was scheduled to meet were awaiting him in his new office. And what's worse, with the way he'd been neglecting his duties lately to be with Syssi, he probably would have to pull an all-nighter to catch up on his work.

Normally, that wouldn't have bothered him, except now, his obligations were eating away at what little time he had left with the woman he loved.

He loved her. No ifs, ands, or buts about it.

Earlier, right after admitting he never wanted to let her go, he'd almost blurted those three monumental words. But letting these words loose when their future was so unclear would've been unkind to Syssi, even cruel.

Choking down that compulsion, his throat had clogged with the unvoiced confession, but he'd covered it well, goofing around with her panties.

When he arrived at the meeting, his sour expression must've forewarned the guys, for once thwarting their usual smart-ass remarks.

Thank fuck.

As he sat down at the table, Onegus took one look at Kian's face and cleared his throat, while Shai busied himself with rearranging the neat stacks of paperwork in front of him. Bhathian only frowned, but that had nothing to do with Kian. A scowl was the guy's regular expression.

"What do we have for today?" Kian asked.

"Carol is back to her old tricks." Onegus pushed his phone over to Kian. "See for yourself; play the recording."

Palming the device, Kian watched the scene playing out on the small screen. Carol, drunk or high on something, sat on a stool with her back propped against the bar, facing a sizable audience. Encouraged by their rapt attention, she went on and on about her adventures as a highly sought after courtesan in eighteenth-century Paris.

Kian sighed. Poor, misguided Carol.

Clearly, it had escaped her notice that as fascinated as her audience had been by the tale she'd been spinning, they had also looked amused. And the fact that they hadn't believed any of it and had thought she was either a nutcase or drunk had been obvious to everyone but her. Nevertheless, she'd broken the law by exposing her impossible age.

"Did you thrall them?" Kian asked Onegus.

"I did. But as she told the same stories the night before, the damage was done."

To most ears, the stories were harmless, too fantastical to be taken as anything but tall tales. But there was a remote chance that their adversaries may hear of it and easily figure out what she was, putting her and the rest of the family in danger.

"Bring her in. The first time she pulled that stunt, I let her off with a warning. But this time, she will stand trial. Let Edna decide what to do with her." Kian sighed, regretting the necessity.

Carol wasn't malicious—just disturbed and not too bright. But he couldn't let her endanger everyone with her behavior. Hopefully, some time spent alone in a small cell would be just the wake-up call she needed.

"Okay, this is settled then." Onegus took his phone back and searched for the next item on his agenda. "Evidently, someone believes that Jackson is thralling girls in his high school into giving him blow jobs. We got this anonymous email last night." He handed the phone to Kian to read for himself.

Bhathian snorted and crossed his arms over his chest. "After the whipping this will earn him, I'm sure blow jobs will lose some of their appeal."

"Jackson is innocent until proven guilty. It may be someone who holds a grudge against him. You know how boys are... and this email was clearly written by a teenager. How old is he anyway? And who does he go to school with?" Kian needed more information before bringing the kid in for questioning.

"He is sixteen, and he is a student at Zelda Mayer's school. We have two more high schoolers there. It is a very prestigious institution, and some of LA's most prominent families send their kids there." Onegus sighed. "It's just getting better, isn't it? What if it was the mayor's daughter or some other public figure's kid? Not to imply that it makes a difference morally, but if she remembers anything and presses charges, it might make the evening news. The cleanup will be a nightmare."

"We'll need to bring our kids in for questioning, all three at the same time. Don't tell them the reason; I don't want them to be able to prepare for it. And what's more important, I don't want Jackson's name smeared because of a rumor. We need to interrogate each one separately to get to the bottom of this." Kian raked his fingers through his hair. If what the email claimed was true, Jackson would stand trial for rape. If proven guilty, he would be sentenced to a whipping.

This kind of punishment seemed barbaric in this time and age, especially when administered to someone who was considered a minor in mortal terms.

But this was their law.

Kids were responsible for their actions as soon as they reached puberty. But although the punishment was just as excruciatingly painful for an immortal as it was for a mortal, the difference was in how fast and fully an immortal healed.

"You know, I got whipped when I was that age. Since then, I've made damn sure that a girl wanted what I was doing to her and never assumed anything again." Bhathian's face contorted in a grimace. "It was a tough lesson, though. I never knew anything could hurt that bad, and I got only two. I hated my mother for a very long time after that; couldn't forgive her for reporting me for something I thought was trivial. She said it was the principle that mattered, and it was better I learned it before doing something worse and earning a more severe punishment."

Hearing this story for the first time, Kian asked, "What did you do?"

"I didn't even thrall the chit. I was kissing her and the kiss got us nice and steamy. She was moaning and clinging to me, so I got cocky and palmed her breast. I thought she was ready for second base, as they call it today. Imagine my surprise when she slapped me and ran to complain to my mother. When I tried to explain that I thought the girl wanted this, my mother saw red. 'Did you ask permission?' she asked. I was dumbfounded. 'Is this what a man is supposed to do? Ask before every move?' I challenged her. She looked me in the eyes and said, 'Yes. You don't have to ask with words, but you ask with your actions. Did your hand linger near her breast, giving her the opportunity to brush it off? Or conversely encourage you to continue? Or did you just go for it?' She was right, of course. Being honest with myself, I knew I didn't want the girl to have the chance to say no, hoping she would like what I was doing and maybe even let me pull up her skirt. So I admitted my guilt, never expecting to get a whipping for my honesty. I was angry for a very long time, but eventually, I understood and internalized how important the law of consent was—mainly after a very embarrassing lecture from my uncle, explaining in graphic detail everything concerning sex. He also explained that my mother was afraid I would not adhere to the law fully unless it were branded into me. I forgave her. But I lost my trust in her. I left home as soon as I was old enough and enlisted in the Guardian force." Bhathian looked down at his hands, his perpetual frown turning into a deep scowl.

Onegus put his hand on Bhathian's shoulder. "We've all done stupid things as kids or gotten punished beyond what we thought was fair. But there is no point in dwelling on past mistakes or the pain suffered, if we learned our lessons and moved on, becoming better people as a result. We are not human, but we are not infallible gods either, regardless of what our ancestors wanted everyone to believe." Onegus squeezed Bhathian's shoulder. "And neither are our mothers. Call your mom, Bhathian. Tell her you love her. It will make you feel better."

"Oh, yeah?" Bhathian arched a brow. "When was the last time you talked with yours?"

Onegus looked down his nose at his friend. "I talk to her every day."

"Seriously, man? You call your mom every day? Isn't that a bit excessive?" Kian blurted.

"You're damn right it's excessive. She calls *me*... several times a day, wants a report on every damn thing I do, keeps me on the phone forever, and gives me a guilt trip when I say I'm busy... You'd think I'm five, instead of five hundred years old..."

Bhathian laughed so hard, his eyes teared. "I didn't know our illustrious commander was a mamma's boy..."

Kian laughed as well, thankful his mother wasn't the intrusive, controlling type. On the contrary, at times when he might have lingered under her protective wing, she had pushed him to become independent, to take more and more responsibility and become the leader she needed him to be.

"Do you think I should talk with Edna about changing the definition of rape in light of your experience? A whipping for getting a feel of a girl's breast seems extreme." Kian had mixed feelings on the subject. Teenage immortals were very hard to control, their new powers lending themselves to feelings of superiority and entitlement. Combined with the impulsiveness and hormonal havoc of their changing bodies, they needed a strong deterrent to keep them from becoming dangerous monsters. Yet, he wished there was an alternative that wouldn't involve such brutal measures.

"And what would you suggest? Not considering nonconsensual oral sex as rape? Sternly scolding offenders for abusing their powers as punishment? Where do we draw the line?" Bhathian surprised them by defending the existing law.

51

Kian conceded, "You're right. Although I would have loved to have a more civilized alternative."

"These laws have served us well for thousands of years. Yes, the whipping is brutal, but the pain starts to recede almost as soon as the punishment ends. The memory of it, however, stays forever, ensuring the perpetrator never dares to repeat the crime. I don't think anything else will work on our kind. The power we have over mortals is too corrupting and too tempting for us not to take advantage of." Bhathian crossed his massive arms over his wide chest.

"He is right. What's the alternative? Keeping teenage offenders locked in the basement for years? I personally would prefer to get whipped and be done with it." Onegus shrugged.

"Let's just hope the accusations are groundless. But if this is the case, we'll need to deal harshly with whoever made them… Anything else on the agenda, Onegus?"

"No, that's all." Onegus got to his feet.

Once the Guardians had left, Kian got up and walked over to the bar, pouring himself a drink before sitting down with Shai to go over the files on his desk. "What's the progress with the resettling?" he asked.

"It's going pretty well, considering the haste. We have all of the Bay Area folks already settled. I hired several services to pack their homes and ship everything to various self-storage facilities around town. The locals are coming in at a slower pace. I estimate at least a month before we are able to drag them all here." Shai smiled apologetically—his initial estimate had been to have everyone settled in less than two weeks.

"The locals are less urgent; it's more of a long term plan. I'm more concerned with the adverse impact of us pulling our programmers out from their respective software firms. We need to figure out a way to enable them to continue their work from here. I need to have a meeting with the programmers and William to work out the logistics."

"I'll schedule it for tomorrow." Shai began fidgeting and rearranging the files, clearly stalling as he gathered his nerve before bringing up the next subject. "As all the council members are already in residence, I thought it might be a good idea to invite them to a nice big dinner. It will be good for morale, a show of unity. I'll take care of all the details. You wouldn't have to do anything other than show up…" Shai was well aware of how much Kian hated entertaining.

"Good idea. When do you have in mind?"

Surprised, Shai looked up. "Tonight… if it's okay with you. It would be best if it looks like something spontaneous that you've just thought of—give the impression that you're actually glad to have them here. I'll have Okidu and Onidu on it. We can use this room, or we can use your dining room; it's up to you." Shai's hopeful expression clearly indicated his preference.

"Having it at my place will be better received. Inform the council members. I also want Syssi and Michael to attend. Let's schedule it for eight. We need to give Okidu enough time to prepare."

Kian heaved a sigh. He was going to hate it. And yet, as regent, this was something that was expected of him, regardless of his lack of skill or enthusiasm for this particular part of the job. And what's more, at a time like this, his family needed to come together.

Pulling out his phone, he texted Syssi and then Amanda, informing them about the dinner.

"Okay, what else do we have?" He glanced at the pile of files Shai had stacked on his desk.

Damn, this was going to take a while.

12

SYSSI

*P*eeking into the dining room, Syssi exhaled in relief. No one was there yet.

Talk about stressful.

As if the prospect of dinner with Kian's posse of Guardians and members of his council wasn't bad enough, he texted her saying he and Amanda were going to be a few minutes late and to go ahead without him.

Great.

It was like inviting your boyfriend's parents to dinner... only worse... because he wouldn't be there with you to greet them.

Imagining the looks and the questions and the judgments passed, Syssi cringed. If she could've thought of any way to wiggle out of it, she would've. Unfortunately, there was a doctor in the house to disprove any pretend maladies she could've come up with. And though the idea of hiding somewhere until Kian showed up crossed her mind, she dismissed it. That would mark her as a coward. Not going to happen. Even though in truth, she was one.

Oh, well, she'd survive.

Shoving her insecurities aside, she turned her focus to the beautifully set table. There was only one way to describe it. Wow.

Okidu had outdone himself preparing for this dinner. Though if that was supposed to be casual, she wondered what possibly more could've been done for a formal affair.

Maybe the butler just didn't get the memo… or got it and ignored it…

He certainly went all out.

Set with fine china, crystal goblets, and what seemed to be real silver silverware, the table looked like something from a period movie. It held the kind of old-world splendor that implied evening gowns and tuxedos. Not jeans.

Everything gleamed, the sparkle bouncing between the expensive-looking stuff on the table and the crystal chandelier above it. Even the artfully folded, pristine white napkins seemed to shine. And the silver goblets, with their tiny though elaborate flower arrangements, must have been delivered fresh from some exclusive florist. No way Okidu could've made those as well.

With a quick look behind her, Syssi pulled her phone out of her back pocket and snapped a picture. The table was so beautiful, she just had to preserve the image.

"Good evening." Onidu startled her as she returned the phone to her pocket.

"Hi, I was just admiring the magnificent table. Was it you or Okidu who set it up so beautifully?"

"It was a joint effort, Madam. And I thank you kindly for your praise. Please, let me show you to your seat." He bowed at the waist and proceeded to pull out a chair for her. The one to the right of Kian's place of honor at the head of the table.

"Thank you." She smiled at him.

As Syssi sat down, the tablecloth's heavy, luxurious fabric brushed against her plain blue jeans, as if to point out that she was underdressed for the occasion. Not that she had much choice in the matter. Besides jeans, her only other option was the black yoga pants she had been wearing when Kian had whisked her to safety. Luckily, she'd at least put on a nice blouse and exchanged her flip-flops for heels.

Good thing she hadn't listened to Amanda's reassurances that it was a casual affair and she didn't need to change.

Yeah, right, casual. Maybe for the queen of England it was!

But then, as the guests began trickling in, dressed just as plainly, she might have relaxed if not for the way they looked at her—as if she was a strange exhibit.

Fidgeting with her napkin, she returned their nods and hellos with a strained, fake smile plastered on her face—all the while secretly plotting revenge on Kian for abandoning her like that.

Except, was it possibly all in her head?

Between the Guardians' friendly, familiar smiles and easy banter, and William's whining about not being seated next to her, she loosened up a bit.

Yeah, it must've been.

And yet, casting a sidelong glance at Michael, she envied the ease with which he seemed to fit in. Calm and confident, his handsome young face smiling, he was chatting with Yamanu and the other Guardians as though they were his lifelong friends.

He seemed happy, excited.

But maybe his good mood had less to do with the camaraderie he felt with his new friends and more with Kri's palm resting possessively on his thigh—publicly staking her claim on him.

Smiling, Syssi looked away from the young couple... Well, one of them was young. Kri, supposedly, was old enough to be Michael's mother.

Oh, well, Syssi shrugged. With an almost two-thousand-year-old boyfriend, who was she to pass judgment.

Boyfriend... the term kind of didn't feel right... whatever... But where the hell was Kian?

Glancing at her watch, Syssi frowned. What was keeping him and Amanda? Most of Kian's guests were already there and waiting for them to show up. Besides theirs, there were only two other vacant spots at the table.

And then even those last two arrived.

One was a frumpy, plain-looking woman; the other a very stylishly dressed, good-looking man. The woman had to be Edna, the judge, but Syssi had no idea who the guy was.

As she contemplated the dichotomy in their appearance, the woman turned her gaze on her, piercing Syssi with pale blue eyes that could only be described as otherworldly. Nailed by that penetrating stare, what Edna or anyone else was wearing became inconsequential.

As she gazed into those unfathomable eyes, everything else in the room seemed to dim and recede into the shadows. Deep, soulful, and wise, they probed her like some alien device, and Syssi had the odd feeling that the woman was reading her thoughts, looking at her memories, and brushing ghostly fingers against her feelings. Unable to look away, powerless against the woman's hold, she was being weighed, measured, and judged.

It wasn't that she felt threatened, there was nothing malevolent in that stare, but she felt violated.

Syssi's distress must have shown on her face because it prompted Edna's companion to come to her rescue. He tapped the woman's shoulder to divert her attention, and as Edna turned to him, he winked at Syssi over her head and smiled.

Released from the woman's hold, Syssi took a deep breath and then another, trying to shake off the uncomfortable tightness in her chest.

But her reprieve was short-lived; the two were heading her way.

"I'm Edna." The woman extended her hand.

Syssi pushed up from her chair. "Hi," she answered coolly. Taking Edna's hand, she concentrated on the woman's neck, avoiding the freaky eyes.

"Sorry about the probe, I know I made you uncomfortable, but it's a knee-jerk reflex." Edna held on to her hand, willing her to look at her face.

"Yeah, well... It was very disturbing to say the least." Syssi took the risk of looking into the woman's eyes again, daring Edna to see how wronged she felt.

Edna held her gaze without flinching and without a hint of remorse. "You're a stranger brought into our fold, and you seem to have our regent ensnared. I had to know what you're about, but I do regret making you uncomfortable."

Syssi's face flushed red. "Find anything interesting?" she asked sarcastically, imagining the kinky stuff the woman had been privy to as she probed her memories.

Unexpectedly, Edna laughed and patted her shoulder. "You're as sweet and as pure as they come, Syssi. But I'm not a mind reader, all I sense are feelings and the purity, or conversely taint of the soul. For whatever it's worth, you have my stamp of approval. I just hope the Fates will treat you kindly." Edna released the hand she was holding and her brief smile wilted, replaced by a look of melancholy contemplation.

"Brandon." Her rescuer offered his hand as Edna left them.

Consumed and shaken by her encounter with his companion, Syssi had forgotten all about him. With a hand over her chest, she exhaled through puckered lips before taking his offered hand. "Hi."

"Just imagine how an accused offender feels under that probe." He chuckled.

"I don't want to. She is scary." Syssi shivered, promising herself to learn and follow every last nuance of immortal law. She never wanted to be judged by those eyes again.

"She is not that bad... after you get used to her soul-searching stare, that is. She is actually an amazing woman. A very harsh and unforgiving one, but a fair judge nonetheless. Not to mention one of the greatest minds you'll ever encounter. Edna is brilliant." He smiled in a disarming yet somewhat overdone manner, making Syssi wonder what he was really like.

"So, what do you do, Brandon? I know everyone else's job here apart from yours."

"I'm the media consultant. The one responsible for our agenda being delivered to the public in enticing pretty packages. Movies, plays, novels... I make it happen. Like an invisible puppet master." He lifted his hands, pretending to be pulling invisible strings with his fingers.

"And what is your agenda?"

"Democracy, equal opportunity, education, human rights, promoting science and technology. To fight evil in all its mired guises; prejudice and discrimination, hatred and ignorance, etc., etc..." Brandon smiled broadly, his white teeth gleaming in a Hollywood-worthy smile that didn't reach his eyes.

Suspecting that under all that easygoing charm, Brandon was a shark in an elegant playboy's disguise, Syssi felt a little wary of him. But then again, she couldn't really fault the guy for having what it took to survive in show business—where the waters were infested with predators.

Good thing that he was using his sharp, shark teeth for the home team. Sharp teeth indeed... Choking on the giggle that was threatening to bubble up, she saluted him. "Well, good for you," she said quickly. "Keep up the good work."

"Will do, ma'am." Brandon grinned.

Finally! She spotted Kian entering the room.

As Syssi's eyes shifted to look at him, Brandon turned around to follow her gaze. "Oh, good, they're here. I'd better take my seat. It was nice chatting with you, Syssi."

"Good evening, everyone," Amanda said as she entered the room with Kian. "Sorry we are a tad late." She took her place to his left.

Kian remained standing at the head of the table, and after a quick smile at Syssi, turned to his guests, waiting for them to hush down. "Good evening, I wasn't planning on making a speech, but I don't want you to get the wrong impression and think this is a party. It seems Okidu and Onidu got carried away in preparing what I intended to be a simple dinner, using this as an excuse to take all this fancy stuff out of storage and finally put it to good use. But this is not a celebration, as it would be inappropriate in light of our recent loss. My plan is to start a new tradition of casual gatherings, once or twice a week, for us to enjoy each other's company as a family, and not just a bunch of individuals working toward a common goal." He paused.

"But as I'm already standing, I would like to take this opportunity to introduce you officially to Michael and Syssi, whom most of you have already met. The credit for finding these two special people belongs to Amanda, who researches mortals with unique paranormal abilities under the assumption that they might be potential Dormants. Syssi has a very strong precognition ability, and Michael is a good receiving telepath. Both agreed to attempt the activation process, which we have already begun." Kian smiled at Michael before resting his eyes on Syssi.

"I would like to propose a toast to a successful outcome of this brave attempt, and the new hope Syssi and Michael bring to our future." Kian raised his goblet, waiting for the others to join in.

Syssi watched with interest the order in which each of those present pushed to their feet to join the toast. Amanda and the Guardians were first, followed closely by William and Bridget. It took a few seconds longer for Edna and Brandon. Evidently, these two still had mixed feelings about the strangers in their midst.

"May the Fates shine kindly upon us and grant us that which our hearts desire." Kian winked at Amanda. With a light squeeze to Syssi's shoulder, he continued. "To all of us—a long, peaceful and prosperous life." He took a long sip of his wine.

"Amen to that!" Michael exclaimed, then looked around the table, puzzled when no one echoed his affirmation. "What?"

"Not many are aware that the term amen actually stems from Amun, the Egyptian god of Thebes," Edna supplied. "With time, his name became synonymous with justice and truth, and hence saying Amen after a prayer or a proclamation served as joining in it and affirming its truthfulness. However, by using his name in this manner, you're implying that you're an Amun worshiper, which I'm sure you're not." She smiled at him apologetically. "I know this tidbit of information tastes sour to most mortals accustomed to saying Amen in their various modes of worship."

"I didn't know that." Michael looked down at his plate.

"Very few do, and even fewer care. It's akin to non-Christians saying, Jesus, or Christ, or atheists saying God. It became just an expression."

Thankfully, the sound of the pantry door swinging open broke the uncomfortable silence that followed.

"Oh, good, I'm definitely ready for some food." Edna unfolded her napkin and draped it over her trousers.

"Dinner is served," Okidu called from under the huge platter of soup bowls he was carrying. With the grace of a seasoned acrobat, he held the enormous thing with one hand while placing the bowls in front of each person without spilling a drop.

How is he doing that? Syssi wondered as she took the first spoonful, closing her eyes when the exquisite flavor hit her taste buds.

For a few precious moments, everyone was quiet, busy with the first course. Then, clearing her throat, Edna addressed Kian. "I don't want to be the Grinch and spoil this festive mood, but aren't we taking a great risk, exposing ourselves this way? I'm not implying that Syssi or Michael's intent is to harm us, but what happens if they don't turn? It will be next to impossible to suppress this many memories. They'll be bound to remember some of it."

"It'll be nothing more than tidbits of hazy dreamlike recollections. I gave

60

it a long and thorough consideration and took a calculated risk, Edna. The alternative is to thrall them repeatedly, which in my experience compounds the damage. And besides being deceitful and cruel, it borders on violating the law of consent, which I'm sure you of all people should find objectionable." Kian held Edna's gaze.

Eventually, she lowered her eyes, reluctantly accepting the logic and moral underpinnings of his decision. "Okay, I agree. I don't like it, but I guess it is a risk we must take."

"Hey, everyone! I have an idea for a movie!" Brandon snapped the tense quiet stretching across the table. "It will be called, *My Immortal Lover*—a love story between an immortal woman and a mortal mercenary soldier who was left for dead and she saves with a small transfusion of her potent blood." With a smug smile, he cast about the dinner guests for support.

"It's so cheesy, I could puke!" Kri didn't hesitate to shoot it down. "I'm so sick of the whole vampire, slash blood thing. How about a bunch of kickass immortal female warriors taking down a drug cartel in Mexico?" She elbowed Bridget, who winced and rubbed her side instead of supporting the idea.

Brandon nodded. "That's actually good… I can see it." He crossed his open palm in front of his face as if painting a picture. "Twelve, tall, scantily dressed, gorgeous women—glistening with the sweat of the hot and humid Mexican air, slaughtering evil drug lords and their merciless minions. They uncover an imprisoned, badly injured group of American commando fighters who had crash-landed in the jungle and been captured by the drug traffickers. They save their lives with injections of their blood, and together they continue the commandos' mission of uncovering and killing an even greater evil: sex slavers, trafficking in young girls."

Brandon flashed Kri his practiced Hollywood smile. "Want a part?" He dangled what he knew she wanted but would never get.

"Hell, yeah! I want a part!" Kri banged her hand on the table. "I can rock a role like that!"

Syssi had to agree. Kri would be perfect portraying an Amazon warrior. "You may have something there. A movie featuring beautiful, scantily clad women bringing justice to the wicked and saving the innocent could become a big box office hit," she said.

"Who would you cast as the main kick-ass girl?" Anandur asked from across the table.

Brandon answered without pause, "There is only one actress I could envision for that part… Charlize Theron." He leaned back in his chair, taking his wine goblet with him.

Anandur's eyes sparkled with excitement. "That's one helluva woman. You can count me in for the lead commando. I want a piece of that…"

"Nice fantasy, children." Kian broke their happy, excited banter. "No one is auditioning for any parts."

"Why not?" Kri whined. "We are all good actors by default; we could pull it off…"

"Don't be stupid, Kri, this whole discussion is absurd."

"It was a fun dream while it lasted." Kri exchanged wistful looks with Anandur.

"By the way…" Kian turned to the doctor. "Do you have any news for us, Bridget?"

"Oh, yes, there is no matrilineal connection. Michael and Syssi are unrelated to us, or each other."

Bridget's announcement should have been good news, and it was. But it was like getting all excited about guessing just one lottery number out of the five—no closer to winning the jackpot than if guessing none.

With that sad realization sinking in, Syssi lost her appetite. Pretending to be busy with the food on her plate, which for all intents and purposes could have been some fast food junk instead of the gourmet meal it was, she tried to swallow. But it tasted like sawdust, clogging her tight throat.

Hiding her somber expression behind the mass of her hair, she hoped Kian wouldn't notice. Sick of her own bouts of sadness, she imagined he was as well.

No one enjoyed the company of a whiny, sad woman.

"It will all work out. You'll see," Amanda said quietly from across the table. "Chin up, Syssi… You too, Kian. A little optimism wouldn't hurt."

The rest of the meal went by quickly, with Kian's palm intermittently finding its way to rest on Syssi's thigh.

After dinner, with everyone stuffed to their limit, Amanda pushed away from the table and rubbed her flat tummy. "Who's up for watching a chick flick with me down at the theater?"

Kian got to his feet and offered Syssi his hand. "You go and have fun, Syssi. I wish I could join you, but, unfortunately, I only made a small dent in the pile of work still waiting for me." He kissed the top of her head.

"Will you be back before I fall asleep?" she whispered, hating the thought of being alone in his big, empty bed.

"The pile waiting for me could take all night to go through, but I don't intend to. Two hours tops. If you're asleep by the time I get there, I'll wake you up... Deal?" He smiled suggestively.

Syssi dipped her head, blushing into his shirt. "Deal."

Kri, Michael, Anandur, and Arwel joined her and Amanda, and together the small group headed for the private theater down in the basement.

With its eight rows of eight plush reclining chairs each, the theater was much larger than Syssi had expected it to be. But then again, this home theater didn't serve an average-sized family; it served a clan.

Sitting down, she engaged the chair's reclining mechanism, turning her viewing experience from merely comfortable to decadent. As the movie Amanda had selected started playing, the quality of picture and sound rivaled that of an IMAX. And that wasn't all. In case someone got hungry or thirsty, a full bar and a popcorn machine were housed in a curtained-off alcove behind the last row. Which was the row Kri and Michael chose, snuggling and kissing like a couple of teenagers.

The romantic comedy had Anandur and Arwel bored in no time. So it was no big surprise when Anandur tapped Amanda's shoulder. "We are leaving to go clubbing, you want to come?"

"No, I'll stay and keep Syssi company," Amanda answered, sounding resigned to her babysitter role.

"Don't be silly, go! I can watch a PG-13 movie all by myself. I promise I'll call you if I need adult supervision to watch an R-rated one." Syssi pushed at Amanda to go.

"Are you sure it's okay?"

"Yes! Go!"

"Okay. Tomorrow at nine, my place. We have a nail appointment scheduled for ten."

"Yes, ma'am!" Syssi saluted and faced the screen, pretending to be absorbed in the movie.

She waited until they left, and then contemplated staying or going up to bed.

The movie was nice enough, but the problem was her acute awareness of the couple necking in the back row. It was hard to ignore their muffled sounds of passion while being the only other person in the theater. She felt like a Peeping Tom, or rather an eavesdropping Tom.

Few moments and several hushed moans later, she pushed up from the comfortable chair, leaving it in the reclining position so the sound of it retracting wouldn't disturb Kri and Michael, and draw their attention to the fact that she was leaving.

13

SYSSI

$\mathcal{A}$s she rode the elevator to the penthouse, Syssi dreaded how empty the place would feel at night. She hoped to at least find Okidu there, except chances were that he was done with the cleanup and already gone.

She wondered where the butler was going each time he disappeared. Was there a girlfriend somewhere? Or maybe he was spending his free time with his brother?

It was hard to tell with Okidu; the man was strange, kind of flat, two-dimensional, like an elaborate caricature instead of a real person. She was saddened by the thought that it might've been the many years of servitude that had painted a permanently false mask over his true self, only allowing him the expressions expected by others.

Syssi sighed. As if she needed another reason to be sad…

Just as she had feared, Kian's penthouse was dark and quiet. Flicking the lights on, she peeked into the dining room and then the kitchen. Amazingly, there was no sign left of the big dinner which had ended only an hour ago.

Walking down the corridor to Kian's room, she paused by each of the closed doors and listened carefully for any kind of sound. But Okidu was either asleep or not there.

The place felt deserted.

Once she reached the master bedroom, a quick glance at Kian's big empty bed convinced her she didn't want to be there alone. And anyway, as strung up as she still felt after that stressful evening, there was no chance she'd be able to fall asleep.

Deciding some quiet time while waiting for Kian was a better plan, Syssi kicked off her shoes and plodded barefoot back to the living room.

As she slid the glass doors open and stepped out onto the terrace, the cool, soft breeze caressing her heated face was refreshing, and with a soft sigh, she sat down on her favorite lounger.

Sprawling comfortably, Syssi took a deep breath and gazed at the clear, cloudless sky, its darkness relieved by the lambent glow of a full moon and tiny sparkling stars. It was peaceful, with the city quiet below and the distant hum of traffic lulling her with its monotone drone. But a few quiet moments later, a tinge of a familiar craving had her glance in the direction of the side table, where she had left Kian's cigarettes.

The pack and his gold-plated lighter were still there, neatly aligned next to a sparkling clean ashtray. Evidently, Okidu had no problem with her little transgression, eliminating the incriminating evidence of the stubbed-out butt, but leaving the pack out there to tempt her.

She looked at it with longing. *Should I? Or shouldn't I?*

It took a few moments of internal struggle, but in the end, she couldn't help herself.

Ah, what the heck...

With a guilty little smile, she reached for the pack, pulled out a cigarette and lit it quickly before her conscience had a chance to talk her out of it. Breathing in carefully, Syssi closed her eyes.

She felt the tension ease out of her with each pull.

Such a decadent pleasure. If only it weren't stinky and unhealthy, she could've enjoyed it guilt-free. The health concern would become a nonissue if she turned, but it wouldn't solve the problem of the clinging stench.

Well, whatever.

Right now, she didn't care. She was alone on the terrace and in her solitude felt free to do as she pleased. That feeling of freedom, the element of rebellion she associated with smoking, was what made the whole thing so delightful—beyond the obvious chemical reaction to the nicotine.

Later, she would just rinse her mouth and spray herself with perfume, and no one would know...

"Hi, gorgeous..." Kian startled her.

Caught red-handed with the cigarette in her hand and smoke coming out of her nose, Syssi felt mortified. How did he get out here without her hearing the sliding door open?

Kian leaned to kiss her.

"Oh, don't kiss me! I stink!" She made a move to stub out the thing.

"No, don't stop on my account!" Smiling, he caught her wrist. "You're obviously enjoying yourself, and I don't mind the smell. They are, after all, mine..." He winked and plopped on the lounge beside her, then pulled out a cigarette for himself. "Now we're going to stink together..." He lit the thing and took a long, grateful pull.

"I wasn't expecting you so soon... you said you'd be working late..."

"That was the plan. But a memory of a certain beautiful, sexy lady was distracting me..." He pulled her panties out of his pocket and brought the crumpled scrap of fabric to his nose. "And these didn't help either..." Kian made a production of inhaling her scent and pretending bliss.

"You're such a pervert..." Syssi laughed.

14

KIAN

"I know..." Kian slanted Syssi a lascivious look. Then remembering Amanda's admonition, stuffed her panties back in his pocket and decided to change topics before their sexual banter got them in bed.

"Did you enjoy dinner?" he asked, then took a puff, exhaling it in a ring of smoke.

"Besides Edna's probe? I guess so."

"Edna probed you? When?"

"Before you and Amanda arrived."

"Shit! I'm sorry, baby, I know how intrusive that feels. What did she say?"

"She liked me, I guess... Gave me her stamp of approval. Not that it mitigated how violated she made me feel. I kept thinking of what she must've seen in my memories—us together, intimate—despite her claim that she can't read thoughts, just emotions. Still, lust is an emotion, isn't it?" Syssi's cheeks reddened all the way up to her ears.

"Whatever she saw, she must have liked it. Don't forget, we don't share mortals' inhibitions about sex. As long as it's consensual there is nothing embarrassing or shameful about it."

"I'm in no way ashamed, but I would like my sex life to remain private.

I'm not into exhibitionism." Syssi stubbed out her cigarette and crossed her arms over her chest.

Kian pushed up from his lounger to sit beside her. Looking at her pouty face, he just couldn't resist her sweet, puffed-up lips and bent down to kiss them. "Imagine you had Edna's ability and were faced with the same dilemma. Would you have acted differently?" He caressed her cheek gently, rubbing his knuckles over her sensuous mouth and along her jawline.

Syssi closed her eyes, kissing his knuckles as they passed her lips, her expressive face flushed with the simmer of arousal stirring up inside her. Then, as if forcing herself to think past her awakening libido, she looked up with hooded eyes as she conceded, "I would have done the same."

Damn, with Syssi responding to him the way she did, it was hard to stick to that whole nonsexual interaction thing. He needed to put some space between them if he had any hope at all of sticking to that plan.

With a sigh, Kian moved to sit on the nearby side table. Facing Syssi, he continued from the safer distance. "Edna is the smartest person I know. I have great respect for her. Actually, she is my second."

"What does it mean, a second, like second in command?" Syssi asked, looking a little hurt, no doubt wondering why he moved to sit away from her.

"No, it's more like a Vice President. She takes over if something happens to me. It should have been Amanda, but she is not ready for that kind of responsibility. Not yet anyway."

Syssi nodded in agreement. "Definitely not... Amanda would have hated it. She told me she was grateful you and Sari spared her the burden."

"That's why I chose Edna. I know she can handle it. Edna is tough, strict, and incredibly capable. Though it's a pity that she is not well liked. Most are wary of her because she seems harsh, and that probing stare of hers doesn't help her popularity either. But I know she is a fair and decent person. A little low on compassion and forgiveness, but nobody is perfect, right?"

"Well, I don't know about that... How about your mother? Isn't she perfect? As a goddess, she must possess incredible power and wisdom..." Syssi's eyes sparkled with curiosity.

Kian chuckled. "Oh, she would like everyone to believe that. She is the ultimate drama queen. I guess that's who Amanda gets it from, though next to our mother, she is an amateur. Annani is incredibly powerful, but she tends to be frivolous, more passionate than contemplative. She might be as smart as Edna, but she is definitely not as wise. Trusting her gut, she acts on impulse, thinking with her heart and not her mind. Surprisingly, it has never steered her wrong, yet. So maybe wisdom is overrated?" He tilted his head, arching his brows.

"What does she look like? Is she majestic and regal?" Syssi was still bursting with curiosity.

"She is. Her power is so palpable, she radiates it." Kian chuckled fondly. "It's funny, though, that all that splendor is housed in a tiny package of a little over five feet, weighing maybe a hundred pounds, half of it probably contributed by her long hair. She could blend in at a high school, posing as a teenager. With her power suppressed, she could pass for a seventeen-year-old girl."

"I have a hard time imagining a childlike goddess inspiring that much awe. Does she believe that she really is a goddess?" Syssi asked.

"Yes and no. She misses the way mortals worshiped her kind and thinks she deserves it. And in a way she does. She is personally responsible for much of humanity's progress. Not to say that mortals wouldn't have eventually done it on their own, but it would have taken them thousands of years longer, and if the Doomers had their way, never. So she deserves her semi-divine status. But of course, we all know that she is not the creator of the universe if such an entity even exists in some form."

"So basically, your kind has no religion? You don't believe in a god?"

"We have no formal religion. There are some festivals and rituals we observe as part of tradition, and we have some informal beliefs. But mostly we are agnostic. Just as mortals, we have limited capacity for understanding the underlying principles of material and nonmaterial existence and, therefore, refrain from making statements regarding things we know next to nothing about. It would be too presumptuous of us to do so based on our infinitesimal knowledge. How about you? What are your beliefs?" Kian asked, despite being afraid of stumbling upon another land mine.

In his experience, mortals clung with irrational ferocity to their faith, no matter how misguided or ridiculous, and felt offended when it was challenged in any way.

"I'm a confused agnostic. I don't believe in a personal, benevolent God who hears our thoughts and answers our prayers. I used to. It was comforting to have that kind of an imaginary friend who was privy to my thoughts, who was always on my side and would always protect me from harm. But as I got older and lost the naive hopefulness of childhood, I could no longer hold on to that belief in the face of reality. I realized that good doesn't always prevail, and very bad things happen to very good people all of the time. Humanity's sordid past and present, the sheer magnitude of suffering, inflicted by both men and nature, does not indicate a benevolent, caring deity. So instead of being constantly angry at that indifferent or even cruel entity, I prefer to think that we are left to our own devices." Syssi paused.

"On the other hand, there is my precognition. How can I get glimpses of a future that didn't happen yet? Or that sometimes I have the feeling that things are fated to happen in a certain way? Or the entire plethora of experiences that could not be explained? Near death visions, messages from beyond the grave... There is just too much of it to be ignored and dismissed as quackery. Do I make any sense?"

Kian pushed up from the small side table to sit back next to her. "Yeah, you do. Amanda believes in fate, and so does my mother. Myself, I'm an old skeptic. But what I know is not to shrug off anything as impossible and conversely not to take anything on faith. There is so much misinformation out there and so little is truly known, regardless of what scientists or religious leaders would like us to believe." His hand was back to caressing her soft cheek, his thumb swiping gently over her tempting lips. He just couldn't stand being near her and not touching her.

Syssi leaned into his palm and placed her hand over his, holding it to her cheek. "Edna said she hoped fate would be kind to me," she whispered. "I have to cling to that hope." She reached with her other hand and pulled him down for a kiss.

Kian bent, twisting his torso so he could press his chest to Syssi's, seeking as much contact as he could from his sitting position.

There was hunger—a desperation—to his kiss that went beyond the physical need relentlessly clawing at him.

He yearned to fuse their kindred souls and cleave to Syssi with the certainty that together they would form something that was better and stronger than the sum of its parts. But at the same time, he suspected that once fused, they would shatter to pieces if forced apart—no longer able to survive on their own.

15

SYSSI

As she held Kian close, running her hands up and down his strong back, a flood of endorphins washed over Syssi, bringing about a profound sense of relief. Clinging to his warmth, inhaling his scent, feeling his familiar hands roaming over her body, she felt as if he was her home, and without him she was just drifting. Rudderless.

It scared her.

Was it just her? Or was falling in love terrifying for everyone? If Kian didn't feel as strongly for her, she'd be crushed. But it was too late to shield her heart.

She was a goner.

Still, to let herself go with that feeling—to revel in it—required the kind of trust she believed existed only between child and parent, and sometimes not even there.

Her body, though, enraptured by the carnality of Kian's kiss, had no problem ignoring the turmoil going on in her head. As he plundered the cavern of her mouth, retreating to nip at her lips, then plundering again, the tiny zings stoked the flames of her desire. And as he moved to the column of her throat, the gentle scrape of his fangs was so damn erotic, it pulled a ragged groan from her chest.

With need unfurling in her belly, she welcomed the familiar tightness in her breasts and the contracting and wet warming of her sex. To abandon herself to her body's cravings felt good, uncomplicated.

Easy to fulfill.

It didn't leave room for doubts or fears.

"I'm taking you to bed…" Kian hissed through his fangs, swiftly snaking his arms underneath her and scooping her up effortlessly.

Curling into his solid body, Syssi smiled. "What took you so long?"

Kian chuckled and dipped his head to kiss her again. "All good things come to those who wait."

"If you say so…" Without realizing it, Syssi had spent the last two years waiting for Kian. She was done waiting, and impatient.

He carried her to his bedroom, stepping inside through the open terrace doors, and put her down on his bed. Taking his time undressing her, he kissed and caressed every inch of skin he was exposing—driving her absolutely crazy.

"Patience, my sweet girl." He pulled her hands away from the jean button she was fumbling with. "I don't want to rush it." He placed her arms at her sides, then kissed her belly before tackling the same button.

Slowly, he unzipped her pants, his lips trailing kisses down her lace-covered mound, but as he stopped right above the juncture of her thighs, Syssi voiced her protest with an angry groan.

Kian lifted his head and smiled an evil, fanged smile before peeling her tight-fitting jeans all the way off her legs.

As her pants hit the floor, Kian paused for a moment to admire what he'd just unveiled, but then as his gaze climbed up to where her pink lace panties were soaked with the evidence of her desire, his eyes lit up and he sucked in a harsh breath.

With hands that trembled with his effort to keep the slow pace he was dictating, he caressed, kissed, and nipped his way up, starting at her toes and culminating at that sweet spot.

Panting with anticipation, Syssi lifted her hips to meet his lips, but Kian would have none of that. Spreading her thighs wide with his hands, he anchored them to the bed, preventing her gyrations. Blowing gently on her hot sex, he cooled it a little, taking his sweet time before finally placing his lips over her small greedy nubbin and kissing it gently through the wet lace.

Syssi was hanging on the precipice. Being held down was turning on the heat, as were his teasing lips, but it was not enough. She needed more and Kian knew it, torturing her with his soft, gentle touches.

He kept alternating between kissing and blowing air on her burning core, denying her what she desperately wanted.

But besides panting, Syssi did nothing to hurry him on. Sensing his determination to go slow, she yielded to his will. And as before, that surrender added another dimension to her pleasure.

Finally, Kian pushed her panties aside and slipped one long finger inside her, groaning when she clenched around it. But his finger didn't move. Holding her still, he pinned her down with his other hand, preventing her from writhing and providing the friction she needed.

Syssi bit down on her lip, struggling to stay still and not plead for him to make her come. But she couldn't stifle the desperate, keening moan that escaped her chest. She was so close. Just a little bit more, and she would go flying.

And still, Kian denied her.

Smiling wickedly, he pulled his finger out and pushed up to kiss her parted lips. "I want you on edge when you take me in your mouth." Climbing higher, Kian straddled her head, then pulled off his shirt and unzipped his pants.

Freeing himself from their confinement, he braced his hand on the headboard above her, looking at her lips as he teased them with the velvety head.

"Open for me," he commanded.

Yes! Syssi closed her eyes, his tone and his words sending a bolt of fiery arousal straight to her sex.

She surprised herself with how much this turned her on; how much she craved taking him as deep down her throat as she could and pleasuring him into oblivion.

Kian went slow, pushing just the crown past her lips. She licked, savoring his taste and the smooth texture of his shaft. He pushed a little deeper, then retracted for several shallow thrusts before going a little farther; careful not to overwhelm her.

When he reached as deep as he could go, he once again pulled out, feeding her just a small portion of his length, making sure she didn't gag.

Syssi moaned around him, in part because she was so turned on, but also because she knew the vibrations would add to his pleasure. No longer restrained, she sneaked her hand to rub at her clit, her hips gyrating in sync with Kian's thrusts.

She was so close, needing just a little more to combust, but the edge eluded her. Kian was getting close as well, hardening and thickening the way he did when his seed was about to burst. And as she prepared for it to flood her mouth and go down her throat, her moans became frantic. Not because she was afraid of how it would feel or taste, or if she would be able to swallow it all, but because she was hungry for it, and the crescendo leading up to the grand finale was driving her wild.

Kian stopped and pulled out.

In seconds, he shucked his pants while she watched—waiting for him with parted lips and heaving chest.

With a growl, he plunged deep into her wet heat.

Syssi was so ready for him that his impressive girth slid effortlessly through her dripping wet folds, denying her the little bite of pain she needed to career over that elusive edge. Still, the way he filled her felt amazing. Arching her back, she urged him to move.

Kian remained still. Buried deep inside her, he waited. "You're not up there with me, yet." He hissed through gritted teeth as he looked into her questioning eyes.

She had no idea what he was talking about. The pleasure was so intense that her eyes rolled back in her head.

But then, as he began rolling his hips, thrusting in and out slowly and forcefully, the pleasure became almost unbearable, and the imaginary rubber band holding her back got pulled taut, reaching its utmost limit.

But Kian held onto his steady pace, not letting it snap.

Bracing on his forearms, he looked down at Syssi's pained expression as he held her mercilessly on the edge—not letting her fly. "I know, baby. I know how much you want to come. But not yet, just a little longer and you'll fly higher than you have ever flown before. And when you come down, I'll be right there to catch you."

Syssi looked up at Kian, her focus splitting between the pulsing and throbbing of the steady push and pull going on below, and the fierce expression on his handsome face. With his eyes glowing again, and his lips peeled back from his elongated fangs, he looked like a monster.

My beautiful monster.

Not letting go of her eyes, he increased the force and tempo of his hammering thrusts and closed his fingers around her taut nipples, gradually increasing the pressure.

Syssi squeezed her eyes shut. It was almost too much, and yet not enough.

But then, as she heard him hiss and felt his fangs pierce the skin of her neck, her eyes flew open and she screamed. The exquisite agony of the twin pricks finally snapping that rubber band.

The orgasm that exploded over her kept coming in wave after wave of pleasure so intense, she felt herself catapult into a different plane.

Coming down, Syssi had no idea how long she'd been out, or which cloud she'd been on while there. Not that it really mattered. She felt at peace, lying encircled in Kian's arms with her face tucked into the crook of his neck, his familiar, masculine scent grounding her in this reality.

"Welcome back to earth, sweet girl." Kian's chuckle reverberated from his chest.

"How long was I out?" Syssi whispered hoarsely, her throat parched and scratchy. She must have been screaming for a while but couldn't remember if she had.

Kian took a water bottle from the nightstand and brought it to her lips. "Here, drink this."

She drank greedily, the water cooling and soothing her sore throat.

"My sweet girl." He kissed her damp temple.

Handing Kian the empty bottle, she curled into his embrace and closed her eyes.

16

DALHU

Sitting in a darkened corner of the nearly empty pub, Dalhu glanced at his phone. It was after two in the morning, and still no word from his men.

After trolling four clubs, he had given up, finding reprieve in this modest establishment. Here he could breathe, as opposed to those bastions of depravity where he'd found the stench of mortals packed tightly like sheep in a pen hard to endure.

It wasn't only the occasional nasty odor of a sweaty, unwashed body—that he could've handled easily. It was the cocktail of other smells mortals produced that had gotten to him—the hormonal outpour of their various emotions—lust and anxiety, greed and envy, rejection and despair, fear…

Nauseating.

And the ogling looks he'd gotten from the females, and some of the males, had disgusted him. No decorum, no modesty. It was Western fetid decay at its worst.

The clubs were brothels and drug dens combined. Except, unlike the brothels, money didn't exchange hands for sexual favors granted or received. The money bought the drugs, and sometimes the drugs also bought the sex. But mostly sex was free.

Except, when it was not. He had spied a few prostitutes working the crowd.

Dalhu took another sip from his drink and shifted in the booth, trying to find a comfortable position for his long legs. The damned thing wasn't built for someone his size.

As it turned out, he didn't have to wait long till texts from his men began coming in, admitting defeat.

Truth be told, he hadn't expected them to succeed. There were hundreds of clubs throughout the big city, and finding an immortal with only seven men on the job was like sifting through rocks at the bottom of a stream—hoping to find gold. Even with the reinforcements due to arrive in a few days it would be more of a miss than hit game.

Where the hell did the bastards go hunting? There must be a way to narrow the search.

Think, damn it.

Where would the privileged sons of bitches hang out? What kind of clubs would appeal to their spoiled sensibilities?

The fuckers were filthy rich—capitalizing on their stolen knowledge and amassing untold fortunes. They claimed it was all in the name of helping humanity. As if getting obscenely wealthy in the process was just a byproduct of their *noble cause*. And as the lucky bastards were known to play nice with each other, everyone got to share in the loot.

They are so full of shit...

They claimed they wanted to bring progress and freedom to the mortals. Freedom from oppression, freedom from hunger, hard labor, discrimination...

What an idiotic and naive notion.

Mortals were not designed to be free. With their herd mentality and the ease with which they were brainwashed by their own leaders and their misguided, blindsided media, it would only take one insane and charismatic ruler to end their world.

Which the bleeding-heart idiots made entirely possible by providing mortals with nuclear know-how.

From Annani's clan perspective, it had been a last resort, desperate move.

The forces of evil, as they had called the Nazis and their cohorts, had been winning the war. Navuh's clever machinations had finally been working, and about to bring humanity's age of enlightenment to a crushing and devastating end.

The clan-sponsored Industrial Revolution, together with the new ideas and philosophies they had promoted, had been threatening to catapult mortals into a new era.

That progress had to be arrested and crushed.

Navuh had maneuvered the events that brought on World War I, and when that war hadn't achieved the desired results, he had easily manipulated the weak and appeasing Western leaders into allowing World War II to go on unchecked while millions had perished.

Humanity had been on the verge of being plunged back into the Dark Ages.

The cataclysmic losses and devastation would've pushed humans back into the arms of their various religions. And those, influenced by Navuh's propaganda, would've blamed the brutal blow on their followers' immoral behavior. They would've zealously shunned their newfound ideas and technology as ungodly and greedy, blaming them for earning their God's wrath.

It had been a beautiful and simple plan that had worked time and again in both enlightened and backward societies.

Humans were so gullible.

But the clan had intervened. They had done the unthinkable, supplying the Allied forces with the tools to develop a nuclear bomb.

For a while, the technology had been closely guarded by the West, but eventually others had gotten their hands on the secret, and now even Navuh's protégés had it.

Funny, how it had come back to bite Annani and her progeny. Their stupidity now threatened to bring their own annihilation.

The virus that had helped bring down Iran's nuclear facilities had only slowed production, as nothing short of a full-out invasion could've brought it to a halt. But by interfering, they had tipped their enemies off.

He had their location. Sort of.

Think! Dalhu commanded himself again. What kind of clubs would the rich go to?

Motioning the waitress over with his empty glass, he placed a hundred dollar bill on the table and pointed to the seat across from him.

"Sorry, honey, as tempting as the offer is, I'm not allowed to sit with customers..." She leaned to wipe the table, offering him a glimpse of her ample cleavage. "It's almost closing time, though. If you can wait, I'd love to, but I don't take money for it..." she whispered throatily.

"The money is for information I need. It will only take a couple minutes of your time... though I'll gladly take your offer for later," Dalhu said quietly, his words coming out somewhat hissed.

She was a pretty little thing, and the thought of fucking her shoved against a wall behind the pub, with his fangs embedded deep in her neck, had his erection and his fangs throb and elongate in unison...

Yeah, that would be very nice... Dalhu readjusted his uncomfortably hard shaft in his pants.

Enjoying his heated reaction, she smiled at him brightly, then turned toward the bartender and lifted two fingers. "Okay, ask. You've got two minutes." As she took the seat across from him, she leaned forward as if to prevent anyone from overhearing their little chat.

"I need the names of the most exclusive nightclubs in LA," he said.

She looked surprised, probably had been expecting something more exciting, but he didn't offer an explanation. It was none of her business.

Scrunching her nose as she tried to come up with the names, she looked cute and very young. Too young to be offering quickies to strangers behind the pub. The thought momentarily tugged at what remained of Dalhu's conscience, only to be shoved aside. She offered herself freely, expecting nothing but pleasure in return.

Dalhu smiled a tight-lipped, cruel smile. That, he could definitely give her, and then some.

It seemed the girl found his nasty smile concupiscent. As the heady scent of her arousal wafted up into his nostrils, her nipples grew visibly taut beneath the flimsy fabric covering her breasts.

She shifted in her seat. "I heard talk about a club named the *Basement*. Personally, I've never been there, nor has anyone I know. It's way, way... out of my league, or yours... Only the rich and famous go there, it's not for regular folks like us." She snorted derisively, crossing her arms over her chest.

"Why would you assume it's out of my league?" Dalhu had taken offense at being bundled in the same category as her. She might be regular people, but there was nothing regular about him. He was one of the finest male specimens of a superior race; the progeny of gods. He wished he could show her. And maybe later he would, just to see her reaction before erasing it from her memory.

"No offense, honey, you're gorgeous… But your Levis and Nikes don't peg you as a potential customer for *The Basement*. These people wear thousand dollar jeans and designer watches that cost more than a new luxury car, not the imitation crap you're flashing." She snorted again, waving a dismissive hand at his Rolex.

"And anyway, you need an invitation from an insider or a lot of grease money to get in. And I mean; a lot of money," she emphasized.

"I guess you're right, it sounds like it really is out of my league. Thanks for the info." He let his lips curve in a tight smile.

"No problem… sorry I wasn't much help. It's just that the clubs I go to aren't fancy, they are for regular people. I could ask around tomorrow, maybe there are some nice clubs that are not that snooty." She pushed up from her seat, hesitating for a spell. "Would you still wait for me? Closing time is only like half an hour away…" Waiting for his answer, she held her breath.

"Sure will, sweetheart…" He winked at her. She was pretty enough, and a free fuck was a free fuck. He was in no hurry.

Watching his little waitress cleaning tables and stacking chairs, he made his plan for the next day. He'd need to go shopping for the type of designer apparel she described and make a bunch of phone calls to see which of his contacts could get him into that club.

Having drug lords and arms dealers as business associates had its fringe benefits. They were exactly the type of people who would value the glamorous scene of a club frequented by the rich and famous.

After all, they happened to be some of the richest people around.

Dalhu grinned, feeling he was on the right track. He shifted to readjust himself again. His damned erection wasn't showing any intentions of letting off, throbbing painfully in the confinement of his jeans. The thing was, he wasn't sure if his hard-on was for the waitress or for his prey. Though, in truth, he had fucked a lot of pretty girls before, but he had never been as close to his coveted prize as he was now.

A little after three in the morning, the girl took her purse, waved the bartender good night, and walked out the door. Dalhu, the only remaining customer, pushed out from his seat and followed her out.

As soon as the doors closed behind them, he had her in his arms, kissing her hard. She moaned and clung to his shoulders as he picked her up and carried her to the alley behind the pub.

Finding a dark recess, Dalhu shoved her against the cold stone, and holding her up with a hand under her ass, pinned her to the wall with his body. Kissing her and licking his way into her mouth, he reached down the top of her flimsy blouse. One at a time, he pulled her breasts out of her bra cups and above the neckline. With both plump globes exposed and pushed up, he took a moment to admire the creamy white flesh, topped by lovely large nipples that were just begging to be sucked. Happy to oblige, he dipped his head, and taking one erect little nub between his lips, lashed it with his tongue.

Panting, the girl closed her eyes and let her head loll back, hitting the wall behind her.

As he feasted, Dalhu groaned in pleasure, sucking, licking and nipping, making sure to give each sweet nipple equal attention. Until it became too much and she pushed at his head. With one last soothing lick to each of the sensitive peaks, he lifted his head to gaze at her pleasure-suffused face. Smug, he then turned to kiss and lick the column of her throat.

She moaned, and her arms slid around his neck, pulling him closer.

He reached under her skirt and pushed her little thong aside, then gently circled her wet folds with his fingers. She almost came when he slid two of them inside, her inner muscles clamping and rippling around his invading digits.

Dalhu stilled, holding her impaled, but not moving them inside her. "Not yet, sweetheart, you'll wait for me," he whispered into her ear, nipping the soft lobe for emphasis.

"Ouch!" she complained, but her sheath stopped spasming. Then as

Dalhu pulled out his fingers to free his shaft, she began writhing against him and closed her eyes in breathless anticipation.

He ripped off her thong and shoved himself inside her with a grunt.

She froze. "Condom! You forgot the condom!" The accusation came out in a loud shrill.

Dalhu froze as soon as she did, but he was actually relieved when she shrieked her accusation, realizing it wasn't pain that caused her alarm.

Looking into her eyes, he released a little thrall, just enough for her to believe that he had taken the necessary precaution. He wanted to keep her lucid for as long as he could.

She relaxed, but her sudden fear had dried out her channel, making it painful for him to move. He forced himself to stay still and take his time kissing her and gently fondling her breasts until she was ready for him again.

Starting with easy shallow thrusts, he stoked her fire, building it up before letting loose and fucking her with wild abandon.

As she neared her climax again, he grabbed her hair and tilted her head to the side, exposing the expanse of her creamy white neck. Licking and kissing the soft skin, he waited for her to reach her peak so he could sink his fangs into her neck while she came. But she was taking too long, and the damned things were throbbing painfully, dripping venom into his mouth and down her neck. He couldn't wait any longer.

With a loud hiss, he struck hard.

As she felt the sharp pain of his fangs slicing through her skin, she gasped and tried to push him off. But it was as effective as shoving at a wall.

Dalhu held her head in an iron grip, keeping it completely immobilized to prevent her from tearing her throat on his embedded fangs.

It took only a few seconds for the venom to do its thing, but it was long enough for the girl to emit the acrid scents of fear and pain.

Fuck! He hated when that happened, cursing himself for forgetting to thrall her before biting her.

Now, it wasn't needed anymore.

As the venom triggered her orgasm, the girl began convulsing around him, and the rippling and squeezing of her tight passage triggered his own happy ending. But the intensity of his climax was diminished by his anger.

Pulling out, he let her down gently, smoothed down her short skirt, and rearranged her breasts inside her bra and blouse.

The lingering euphoria kept her docile and weak. If not for his hand holding her up, she would've crumpled to the alley's floor like a rag doll.

"Look at me," he commanded, curling a finger under her chin and tilting her head up so she was forced to look into his eyes. Very carefully, Dalhu sifted through her most recent memories, changing and erasing only the small portion needed to protect his identity and the memory of the bite. Fortunately for her, he was old enough and experienced enough not to do the hatchet job a younger immortal would have done.

Still, the girl looked dazed.

He had to make sure she arrived home safely.

There was no way he was just going to leave her in her dazed and confused state alone in the dark alley. A woman alone in the middle of the night was vulnerable, even with all her faculties intact.

If anything should happen to her, someone might remember him leaving the pub with her. And that wouldn't be good.

Glancing at her parted lips, Dalhu suddenly felt a need for one last taste and dipped his head to kiss her. He had forgotten how damn good it felt to have a woman because she wanted him, and not because he paid her to pretend she did... "I'll walk you to your car." He wrapped his arm around the girl's waist and led her toward the pub's parking lot.

Holding her tightly against his side, as they crossed the short distance to her car, Dalhu wanted to feel contempt for her, and to some extent he did. She was a slut—offering herself like this to a complete stranger.

He was taught to believe that decent women were only supposed to service their husbands, with prostitution being a necessary evil that was tolerated only for the sake of single men like him.

Except, he found he couldn't harbor negative feelings for the fragile and vulnerable girl leaning on him for support.

She fumbled with her key, having a hard time inserting it into the handle of her old, beat-up car. He took them from her, helped her get in, and buckled her seatbelt around her, then dipped his head and kissed her swollen lips for the last time.

"Wait until you feel okay to drive," he said before closing her door.

85

Walking over to the only other car still parked next to the pub, Dalhu folded his six-foot-seven-inch frame into the driver seat of his rented Mercedes. The luxury car engaged automatically, but he didn't drive off, waiting for the girl to exit the parking lot first.

She wasn't safe yet. Some scumbag might be lurking in the shadows, just waiting for Dalhu to leave her unprotected.

He hated those kinds of worms.

It was ironic really; on a battlefield, he was a cold-blooded killer but wouldn't let harm come to a female if he could help it. Only cowards and scum preyed on women and girls, and when facing someone like him, the same maggots who relished the power of abusing the weak and defenseless would cower and piss themselves.

They didn't deserve to live.

Tightening his hands on the steering wheel, he felt the familiar rage rising and wished like hell for one of the worms to show himself so he could kill the bastard. His eyes glowing with his seething anger, he scanned the area for any signs of a potential perpetrator, letting his senses spread out over everything in his surroundings. But besides the two cars idling in the parking lot, the place was deserted.

Fuck. Now he was stuck with his rage engaged and no one to take it out on.

A few minutes later, the girl finally pulled out into the street and drove away. As her car disappeared around the curve and he shifted the transmission to drive, Dalhu realized he hadn't even asked her for her name.

17

KIAN

"Kian! Are you even listening?" Onegus asked.

The morning meeting had been going on for some time, but Kian was barely paying attention to Onegus or any of the other Guardians present.

Ever since waking up before sunrise and reluctantly extracting himself from Syssi's warm embrace, he'd been preoccupied with thoughts of her.

Despite the mountain of work he'd planned to catch up on before the meeting, he'd spent most of the time leaning back in his chair and ignoring the stuff on his desk.

He found himself grinning like a fool, recalling pieces of their conversations—her smiles, the desire in her eyes, the way she responded to him. The sexy sounds she made. But most of all, he cherished the way she would on occasion look at him adoringly, as if he was the most wonderful man in the world. And in those moments, he could almost believe it.

She made him happy.

He loved her.

And imagining life without her was unbearable.

Kian's smile wilted, and as a tidal wave of emotions swept over him, grabbing at his heart and squeezing hard, he clutched at his chest—the hoping, the wishing... imploring the fates and the gods and whoever else might heed his plea...

She had to turn. He'd go insane if she didn't.

Then it hit him.

If he waited until after her transition to tell her he loved her, she would always doubt his sincerity. Becoming the most valuable asset to him and his clan, she'd believe he would do and say just about anything to keep her—regardless of his true feelings.

He needed to tell her now. Even if it meant more pain down the road if she didn't turn. Syssi deserved to hear him say it, out loud. His love not just implied but voiced clearly and emphatically.

Decided, Kian felt almost giddy with anticipation. He'd tell her tonight at dinner; the exclusive restaurant providing the perfect romantic setting. And what's more... he'd get to say it out of bed. The last thing he wanted was for her to think he said the words in the throes of passion without giving it real thought.

If he was to proclaim his love, he wanted to do it right, without leaving even a shred of doubt in Syssi's mind as to how deep and encompassing his love for her was.

"Kian?" Onegus snapped his fingers in front of Kian's face.

"Sorry, could you repeat what you've said? My mind was elsewhere."

"Was it by any chance preoccupied with a certain young lady? The one peeking at you from behind the glass doors?"

Kian looked up, and there she was, his sweet Syssi. Standing outside the conference room's closed doors, smiling at him and doing the little wave thing with her hand.

"Please excuse me for a moment. I'll be right back." Kian pushed out of his chair and in long, urgent strides hurried toward his love.

18

SYSSI

*U*nnerved by Kian's intense gaze and stalking stride, Syssi took a step back. Was it a mistake to come here uninvited and intrude on his meeting? Was he angry with her?

She just wanted to see him and say goodbye before leaving for her shopping trip with Amanda.

But then, as soon as the French doors closed behind him, he lifted her in his arms and kissed the living daylights out of her.

Lost in the passionate kiss, she closed her eyes until the sounds of catcalls percolating through the closed doors reminded her they had an audience.

Kian was kissing her in clear view of everyone in the conference room—as if staking his claim in a public declaration of ownership.

Her embarrassment cooling some of her fervor, Syssi pushed ineffectually at the solid wall of his chest.

Growling at her in warning, he tightened the grip on her nape and deepened his kiss.

Their audience forgotten, Syssi felt like any moment now Kian would tear off her clothes and have his wicked way with her right there on the floor. But instead of alarm, the thought sent delicious shivers of desire through her, and she clung to him, moaning into his mouth.

Kian broke the kiss only when their oxygen ran out; he then turned to look at the Guardians' smirking faces behind the glass doors, giving them a look that sent a clear message.

This is my woman!

Holding Syssi in his arms, he took two steps to the right and out of the Guardians' line of sight. With a big grin on his beautiful face, he pressed her against the wall next to the doors.

Syssi giggled. Kian looked kind of conceited—like a warrior returning victorious from battle and claiming his reward by ravishing his woman.

Heck, yeah, he is welcome to ravish me anytime.

Wrapping her legs around him, she clung to him, and holding on like a monkey, peppered his neck and his chin with urgent kisses before attacking his lips.

With his hands freed from holding her up, Kian brought his palm to her cheek, caressing it tenderly until she relinquished his mouth to look into his eyes.

They were glowing, and the ferocity she saw in them would've been scary if not for his tender caress.

"You're mine," he growled, a shadow of trepidation crossing his eyes.

Did he think she would object? Wasn't it obvious?

Then it dawned on her. The sweet man wasn't sure and needed to hear her acquiesce.

Pulling her courage around her, Syssi gave him what he seemed so desperate for. "I'm yours," she whispered, her voice shaky with her own fear of baring her soul. "But are you mine, Kian?"

"Body and soul, my love." Kian's eyes shone with tender emotion, their fierceness softened by his feelings.

"What are you saying?" Syssi whispered, her throat tight as she struggled to hold back the emotional storm threatening to erupt.

"I'm saying that I love you, my sweet Syssi." He sighed. "I had it all planned… wanted to tell you tonight over a romantic dinner… But instead, I had to blurt it out here, in the drab corridor of our basement, with you pushed against the wall. I'm such a fucking moron." He dipped his head and touched his forehead to hers.

"I will not allow you to talk this way about the man I love. You hear me?"

Syssi pretended to scold him while her heart was overflowing with feeling. Stroking his silky hair with both hands, she waited until he chuckled softly.

"I don't need romantic gestures, Kian, or fancy dinners to charm me into loving you." She cupped his cheeks with her palms and pulled his head up so he could see the truth in her eyes. "Those are nice, and I appreciate the thought and the effort, but I don't need them. This… raw and true, in its naked, unadorned essence… this feels right. Something perfectly timed and staged, but lacking in ferocity just can't compare. I love that you feel so strongly about me that you couldn't hold it inside for a moment longer. You couldn't have done it better if you'd tried."

Kian smiled, his whole face brightening. "You must truly love me to think so." He shook his head in disbelief.

"You really love me…" he repeated in a whisper.

Didn't he know? Or was he just happy to hear her say it?

"Of course I love you, silly boy. Didn't I show you? Couldn't you tell?"

"Yes, but I had to be sure. Under this guise of confidence, I'm just as insecure as the next guy." He chuckled, pretending to exhale a relieved breath and wipe some imaginary sweat from his forehead.

"I love you… I love you… I love you…" Syssi laughed, planting sloppy kisses all over his face between one I-love-you and the next. "Now let me go before Amanda blows a gasket. She's been waiting in the limo this whole time. We can continue later over that romantic dinner you promised me…"

"Okay." Kian let her slide down his body, making sure she didn't miss the bulge in his pants on her way down. Then held on, not ready to release her yet. "You're mine, don't forget it…" He kissed her until her toes curled and she forgot all about Amanda.

19

SYSSI

"You very pretty lady, still no husband?" the tiny Vietnamese asked in heavily accented English, her old face scrunched in a disapproving grimace.

Sitting on her stool at Amanda's feet and applying bright red nail polish to her toes, she somehow managed a regally condescending attitude from her low perch.

The small nail salon wasn't at all what Syssi had been expecting. Instead of an elegant and snobby Beverly Hills spa, Amanda had taken her to this everywoman's place, smirking at Syssi's surprised face.

"They are hilarious," Amanda said in a hushed voice. "It's like watching a comedy show while having your nails done. I love it here. The women are all from the same family and they entertain themselves by poking fun at each other and at the customers. They are shameless, especially when they think no one understands what they are saying..."

"Where did you learn Vietnamese?" Syssi whispered back. "And what the heck for?"

"I know a little, just enough to converse. Or eavesdrop. I pick up languages easily..." Amanda trailed off.

"She so pretty, no man good enough, huh?" The younger woman buffing

Amanda's nails arched her eyebrow like a scolding schoolmistress, then winked at the old crone at Amanda's feet.

"Maybe I don't like men?" Amanda taunted.

The woman's jaw dropped. And with her brown eyes peeling wide in mock shock, she snorted, saying something in Vietnamese that had all the others guffaw. A fast exchange and more laughter followed.

"What are they saying?" Syssi asked the young woman massaging lotion into her hands.

"Oh, they say she lie, she a man-eater. Like the tiger say he no like meat. They say, one man no enough food, she need many." The girl smirked.

"Wow, Amanda, they got you pegged. I wonder what tipped them off?" Syssi slanted a look at her friend.

"I'm telling you, they are witches... They're probably hiding a smoldering cauldron somewhere in the back, and every time they disappear over there, they toss our nail clippings into the pot and chant spells to spy on our lives and discover all of our secrets..."

"Maybe a husband for you in pot, I go see, maybe tell you if he handsome, maybe no." The old crone cackled.

"You see why I love them? They have a sense of humor and are not afraid to use it." Amanda blew a kiss at the old woman who was smiling smugly at her toes.

"Next, Rodeo Drive," Amanda said as they exited the hair salon, which in contrast to the nail place had been just as fancy and snobby as Syssi had been worried it would be. But she had to admit, her hair had never looked better. Without shortening it, or changing its natural wave, the hair designer with delusions of grandeur had made it look sophisticatedly tamed.

The makeup job, however, had been what really had blown her away. Armando, the self-proclaimed makeup artist to the stars, was a magician. Looking at herself in the mirror, she'd followed his magic taking shape on her face with a wide-eyed stare. He'd made her look stunning. Examining herself from various angles, Syssi had grinned at her reflection in the mirror. Kian's jaw would drop down to his chest when he saw her tonight.

"You're gorgeous, darling. Go get 'em, girl." Armando had shooed her up from the chair, making room for his next customer. "Kiss, kiss." He'd kissed the air next to her cheeks and hurried to escort to his station a very elegant lady, whom Syssi could've sworn she'd seen somewhere before... Maybe on TV?

"Wait till you see the outfits Joann picked for you to try." Amanda had called ahead, giving Syssi's measurements to the proprietor of her favorite boutique. "She has excellent taste and connections in all the top designer houses. Prepare to be wowed."

"Don't get your hopes up. I have a real hard time with dresses. They never seem to fit right." Syssi made a pouty face. "I usually end up with a skirt and top."

"Don't worry, they make fabulous alterations. Everything is going to fit perfectly." Amanda opened the door to the exclusive boutique, motioning for her to step in.

"Amanda! Syssi! Come in. I have your selections in the back room." Joann gave each a perfunctory hug before ushering them into the large, private changing room.

Mirrors everywhere, the room was furnished with two white couches, probably provided for those who wished to watch the clothes being modeled on the small raised stage.

"Wine? Cappuccino? Mineral water?" she asked, striking a well-practiced pose. At one time, Joann must've been a model—rail-thin, perfectly groomed, and beautiful—she made quite an impression.

"Wine sounds good." Amanda walked over to check out the outfits Joann had prepared for them to try.

"Syssi, this must be for you. The thing is too short to cover my butt." Amanda handed her a tiny dress.

"Is this supposed to be a dress? It looks like a swimming suit." Syssi pulled the stretchy fabric, trying to figure out how it could cover her.

"Yeah, it looks kind of small... But I trust Joann. Just try it on."

Amanda had been right. Every dress, skirt, and blouse Syssi had tried on looked amazing on her. It was difficult to narrow it down to one outfit.

"I need help, Amanda! I'm going crazy trying to decide which one looks the best. You've got to help me choose," Syssi beseeched, looking over the large selection again.

"Easy, we take them all. Joann, can you find shoes to go with Syssi's outfits?" she addressed the proprietor, ignoring Syssi's vigorous side-to-side head shaking.

"No way I'm taking all of it! That's tens of thousands of dollars in merchandise! Are you out of your mind?" Syssi's voice rose with each word, becoming shrill.

"Ignore her protests." Amanda waved the perplexed Joann away and turned to confront Syssi.

Syssi's face felt so hot, she was certain she was flushed all the way from her chest to the roots of her hair. And the way she was hyperventilating got her so choked up, she couldn't speak.

Which, of course, Amanda took advantage of, plunging right ahead with her campaign. "Look, sweetie, don't get so upset. You cannot continue prancing around in your plain T-shirts and jeans that you bought at Macy's on sale. Not after what Kian did today; it would reflect badly on him. You have no choice."

Amanda succeeded in stunning her out of her anger. "How do you know what he did today? You weren't there... And anyway, what does it have to do with what I wear or don't wear?"

"Kri texted me and probably every other female in the clan. It's huge news and it travels fast when our regent not only falls head over heels in love but makes it public. I'm so happy for you both, I could cry." She wrapped her arms around Syssi, hugging her tightly and sniffling. "It's so romantic..." She sighed dramatically, adding another sniffle for effect before letting go.

"I can't believe you knew and said nothing until now. And how the heck did Kri hear us? We were outside in the hallway and the doors were closed..." Feeling exposed, Syssi crossed her arms over her chest.

"You forget how exceptional our hearing is, everybody heard. And I didn't say anything because I waited for you to fess up. Some best friend you are—not telling me right away." Amanda pouted and folded her arms over her chest as well.

"I can't believe everyone heard, it should have been private." Syssi let her chin drop, disappointed at having her cherished moment shared with a crowd. Then a suspicion had her pin Amanda with a hurt look. "Kian knew, didn't he? This whole thing was some caveman-like display of ownership to warn off the other guys, wasn't it?" she asked, her doubts and insecurities raising their ugly heads.

"No, sweetie, don't you dare belittle what transpired between you two, just because it was witnessed by people who happen to care a lot about Kian and about you. I don't think it even crossed his mind." She chuckled at Syssi's arched eyebrow. "Not the toe-curling kiss, that he wanted everyone to see. He was making a statement... I mean the things he said after... when you were alone and out of sight. He got carried away, forgetting he had an audience. Give him some credit, would you?"

"Yeah, you might be right... It's just... I feel like something was stolen from me... I was so happy..." Syssi wiped at the traitorous tear sliding under her eye.

"I'm so sorry, darling. I should have kept my big mouth shut. The last thing I wanted to do was to upset you. You know that I love you, right?" Amanda dipped her head to peek into Syssi's downcast eyes.

"I'm sorry too. I don't know why I'm so emotional..." Syssi heaved a breath and tried to crank up a smile.

"Are you kidding me? You are taking it all like a trouper. Your whole life has been turned upside down. You fall in love, and you're facing the possibility of becoming immortal... I'm surprised you didn't crack till now. I would if I were you." Amanda embraced her once more, caressing her back in small circles.

"Thank you. You're a really good friend, you know?"

"I know... but wait till you see how I do as a sister-in-law..." Amanda chuckled and started singing quietly in Syssi's ear: *Love and marriage, love and marriage go together like a horse and carriage. This I tell you brother, you can't have one without the other.*

"What's next? You'll start going around singing; *Kian and Syssi, sitting in a tree?*" Syssi laughed, feeling better despite herself.

"I just might..."

20

ANDREW

ndrew was early—the precaution of arriving ahead of time to stake out a place a deeply ingrained habit he saw no reason to forgo just because of his shift to civilian life. Selecting a table facing the front, he watched the glass door, waiting for his first peek of the infamous professor.

He had expected Dr. Amanda Dokani to be good-looking—Syssi mentioned the woman was stunning... once or twice... or a hundred times —but nothing could have prepared him for the sight of the most beautiful woman he had ever seen, on-screen or off, walking in behind his sister and towering over Syssi's slight form.

She must've topped six feet, all of it exquisitely shaped and expensively dressed. And her short, almost boyish haircut did nothing to detract from the perfection of her beautiful, feminine face.

His jaw literally dropped before he willed it shut and swallowed the drool that had gathered in his mouth. Pushing up from his chair, he smoothed his hair and pulled on the lapels of his suit jacket, making sure they lay flat—suddenly mindful of his appearance.

For the first time in his life, Andrew felt inadequate and it pissed him off.

He managed a smile for Syssi, who left her gorgeous boss behind and rushed to give him a hug with a big grin on her face. He was thankful for the reprieve his sister's hug was affording him, using it to collect himself as he waited for Amanda to catch up. Glancing over Syssi's shoulder, he watched her saunter with a sensual sway to her hips, carrying her body with the confident glide of a graceful predator.

She caught him staring at her and held his gaze with a small, devious smile curling one side of her full, luscious lips.

Letting go of Syssi, he extended his hand and forced a well-practiced smile on his face. "Hi, it's a pleasure to finally meet you, Amanda. Syssi told me so much about you." Andrew smiled, satisfied that his tone hadn't betrayed how nervous she made him feel.

"The pleasure is all mine, Andrew," she purred, her incredibly blue eyes twinkling with coquettish amusement as she took his offered hand, leaving her elegant, long fingers in his grasp.

Andrew was intrigued. He had little experience of being pursued; his severe demeanor discouraging most women, to the exclusion of the gutsy or the clueless, from making a move. And as he wasn't a rich man, and in his own opinion not that good-looking, there was hardly a reason for any to make an effort. Which meant that he was used to being the hunter and couldn't decide whether he liked this reversal of roles or not. On the one hand, he was flattered and turned on. On the other, he felt uncomfortable and suspicious when a woman like that gave him this kind of attention. Not that he had ever met a woman like Dr. Amanda Dokani.

As they waited for their food, Andrew felt Amanda's eyes watching him and pretended not to notice, keeping his gaze firmly on his sister while they chitchatted about their parents' recent adventures in Africa.

He feared that once he shifted his eyes to her, he would get stuck gaping at her beautiful face like an awestruck, pubescent boy.

Later, when their lunch arrived, he waited for Amanda to focus her attention on her food so he could ogle her without being observed. But somehow, the damn woman ate without looking at her plate and kept pinning him with that sexy gaze of hers. And if that wasn't enough to make him sweat, she was driving him nuts with the way she ate, each sensually infused bite sending a signal straight to his groin.

She was toying with him, tantalizing him, and deriving wicked satisfaction from his discomfort.

Experiencing this new and unexpected chink in his armor was making him angry, which in turn helped him regain control. He was nearly forty, and a Special Forces veteran for fuck's sake, not a goddamned horny teenager.

Time to switch things around and shift the direction this campaign is going.

Placing his napkin over his plate, he lifted his glass of mineral water and leaned back in his chair, staring straight into Amanda's deep blue eyes.

"I have a few questions for you, Amanda. I hear Syssi is involved with your brother, and as she refuses to let me check him out, she leaves me with no other choice but to grill you instead. What could you tell me about him? What kind of a man is he?" Andrew ignored Syssi's sharp kick to his shin.

Amanda looked surprised by his question, evidently not expecting him to be able to focus on anything other than her magnificent self. As she mulled over her answer, a couple of moments passed before she said, "He is smart, loyal, hardworking and cares a lot about Syssi... Does that answer your question? It's all true. But how can you trust my word? After all, he's my brother and I'm biased..." She smiled innocently and took another tantalizing bite of her sandwich.

"I have no reason to doubt you. All I wanted was your honest opinion... Any negatives you'd care to share?" Andrew smirked smugly, noting her questioning eyes. She'd anticipated he wouldn't take her word at face value, but he always knew when people were lying to his face, and Amanda was telling him what she believed was the truth.

"Well, not many... He works too hard, is way too serious, doesn't know how to let loose and enjoy himself, and has a short fuse... probably because he works too hard and doesn't let loose... So although I love him, I find him somewhat boring and sometimes overbearing, but Syssi's opinion of him differs, doesn't it, sweetie?"

Amanda glanced at Syssi fondly, her whole face softening. Impossibly, she became even lovelier as she momentarily dropped her seductress act, and some of her true self shone through the facade she was projecting.

Andrew smiled. Amanda regarded his sister like a cougar would regard her cub. Which was funny—such a motherly, protective expression coming from someone so young.

Syssi's face reddened as she tried to come up with an answer, probably afraid to sound like she was waxing poetic about her new boyfriend. "I find him fascinating, charming, and sweet." She dug into her food with gusto, refusing to look Andrew in the eyes.

By the deepening crimson of her cheeks, he could just imagine the things she'd left unsaid.

Chuckling at his sister's obvious discomfort, he shared a knowing look with Amanda—feeling an odd affinity with her. She seemed not much older than Syssi, but there was something about her that made him think of her as someone closer to his age. Maybe it was life experience, or perhaps her title, that made her seem older, more mature... or maybe it was his wishful thinking. He needed Amanda to be at least thirty so he could lust after her without feeling like a dirty old man.

Later, as the topic of conversation shifted to what had happened at the lab and then to Amanda's research, she dropped her femme fatale persona for good, becoming the consummate scientist instead. And the passion she had for her work impressed Andrew in a way her previous antics did not.

21

AMANDA

The change in Andrew's guarded demeanor had not escaped Amanda's notice, and she realized that her earlier efforts to make him squirm had been the wrong approach.

She'd been coming on too strong.

Some men were just strange that way; offended instead of grateful for being pursued by a beautiful woman. Or maybe he wasn't used to this kind of attention. Except, if that were the case, she couldn't understand what kept her competition away. He was very attractive in his own rugged and brooding way.

Tall and broad, his handsome if not pretty face was adorned with two small scars; one slicing diagonally across his chin, and a smaller one over his left brow. In her opinion, the scars only added character to his irresistible bad-boy allure. She wondered if there were any more of these cruel testaments to the battles he'd fought and survived hidden beneath the cover of his clothes. It was despicable of her, but she hoped so. It would make him even yummier…

There was nothing like a fierce warrior to whet her appetite…

Now that she'd eased up on the sexual innuendo, he seemed to be really taken with her, the scent of his arousal intensifying as he let down his guard. The dear man was attracted to her intellect and not just her looks.

How sweet. It made her like him even more.

It was a shame she couldn't just drag him off somewhere private and show him how much. But there was something she needed to do away from Syssi and her yummy brother.

Amanda sighed. "As much fun as this is, I have a few more errands I have to run. You two stay. No reason to cut your time together short on my account." Pushing up from her chair, she collected her handbag. "Onidu is parked in the back and will take you home when you're ready."

"What about you?"

"I'll call him when I'm done to come and pick me up, or maybe I'll just take a cab home." Amanda leaned to kiss Syssi goodbye. "Andrew, it was a pleasure. Once the lab is up and running again, I would love to run a few tests on you as well, if you're willing of course."

Andrew stood up and offered his hand. "Sure, it would be my pleasure. Just let me know when. I had a really good time... You're a fascinating woman, Amanda."

Ignoring his offered palm, Amanda pulled him in for a quick hug and kissed his cheek. "We're family now, shaking hands is for strangers." Flashing him her megawatt smile, she chuckled as a blush crept up his rugged face.

Once out of the café, Amanda walked the short distance back to the shops, heading for a jewelry store.

She planned to have a duplicate made of the small heart pendant hidden behind the collar of her blouse—the one Syssi had given her. There was no reason for Andrew to get upset upon discovering that Syssi had given away his gift. With both of them having identical pendants, chances were he would never find out.

2 2

DALHU

*D*alhu stuffed his shopping bags in the trunk of his rented car, still outraged at the obscene cost of the few items they contained. Two pairs of designer jeans at over a thousand dollars each, and a dress shirt at close to eight hundred—insane—he'd bought three.

Not to mention the custom tailored suit he'd ordered for six thousand four hundred dollars. And this was supposed to be a great deal. After over an hour of bargaining, he'd managed to get it at half the price he'd been quoted, the timid tailor probably giving in out of fear.

That still left the shoes.

Damn! He hated shopping.

It seemed as if all the high-end mens apparel boutiques were operated by faggots. And not the kind that kept their sexual orientation to themselves. No, he had to be served by the flamboyant types; getting drooled on in one store and fondled, *accidentally,* in another.

The guy was probably still nursing the offending hand… It had taken supreme effort on Dalhu's part to refrain from crushing it to dust.

The things he had to endure for his job…

Leaving the car parked behind the restaurant he had lunch at, Dalhu headed back to the war zone of the shopping jungle.

With the shoe store across the street in mind, he walked over to the crosswalk and waited for the lights to change at the intersection when a tingling at the back of his neck made him turn his head and look to his right.

His attention was immediately drawn to a tall, exquisitely shaped female walking away from him. And as he kept staring at her retreating back, Dalhu felt a shiver of awareness and a hint of recollection.

Everything else forgotten, he hurried to shorten the distance between them, careful not to get too close.

He needed to see her face.

There was something familiar about her tugging at his memory. Perhaps she was a movie star, or a model he recognized from the screen or from a magazine. Either way, he had to find out.

The woman stopped in front of a window display, and he had no choice but to pass her by. Pausing to stand beside her would have been too conspicuous. There weren't that many people walking down the street, and with his height and build it was impossible for him to blend in—even in a crowd.

Passing several stores, he ducked into the first one that wasn't exclusively geared toward women and displayed a decent selection of luxury watches for men. Pretending to look around, he had his eyes on the street, waiting for her to walk by.

A few minutes later, he grew anxious. She'd either turned back or had gone inside the store with the window display she had been admiring before. But as he stepped out, intending to backtrack and pick up her trail, he was relieved to see her a couple of storefronts down, looking at another display.

Good, she was still heading his way.

Glimpsing her profile, he was certain he'd seen her before. Something about this magnificent creature made his stomach churn with excitement. And it wasn't just a male's natural response to an attractive female. For some reason, he had a feeling about her...

A very good feeling...

With his muscles coiled and ready to pounce, Dalhu retreated into the darkened interior of the watch store and waited.

It was his lucky day...

She walked in.

As her eyes landed on him, she froze, the rising terror on her beautiful face indicating that her mind had just finished processing what she had already felt in her gut.

In that moment of recognition, two lightning-quick realizations hit him at once. First, he knew who she was. She had cut her hair short and colored it black, but there was no mistaking the stunning face he knew so well from the framed picture he kept by his bed. Second, he was going to grab her and run.

Fate had granted him this one chance to have a shot at fulfilling all of his impossible dreams, and he was going to take it. But he had to act fast.

The professor was about to bolt.

23

AMANDA

manda was paralyzed with fear. Aside from one girl behind the counter, she was alone with a huge Doomer in the jewelry store.

There was no doubt in her mind as to what he was—the scent of his arousal was distinctly that of an immortal male... and not one of her clan.

Run, she commanded her feet, but they took too long to respond.

She was too late.

As she turned to flee, her fight-or-flight response finally kicking in, he lunged for her and grabbed her neck.

"Don't move, and don't make a sound if you want that girl to live," he whispered in her ear.

"Is everything okay?" hesitantly, the girl asked from behind the counter—hopefully, with her finger hovering over the panic button.

"Everything is all right. Don't worry about it. It's just a game my girl-friend and I play." He projected influence with his voice, which Amanda prayed wouldn't be enough to thrall the girl without him looking directly into her eyes.

Obviously not possessing the strongest of minds, the girl said cheerfully, "Okay then." She shattered Amanda's last sliver of hope.

Desperate and scared out of her mind now that she realized the Doomer could also effect a powerful thrall, Amanda began shaking in his grasp.

"Don't be afraid," he whispered, his mouth so close to her ear, his breath tickled. "I mean you no harm." He slackened his grip on her neck and blew warm air on the bruised area. Moving his large hand around, his strong fingers closed over her throat and chin.

Tilting her head, he struck quickly, sinking his fangs into her neck.

I'm going to die, was the last coherent thought Amanda had before the venom-induced pleasure took over her body and mind.

She leaned back into the strong male behind her, marveling at how nice it felt to be held by someone so much taller than her for a change. He smelled delicious, all male and fresh scent of soap. And as her body flushed with powerful arousal, she wanted him to touch her all over.

Arching her back, Amanda mentally willed him to bring his big hands up and cup her aching breasts. She pressed her behind into his groin, rubbing against his erection. "Just touch me before I die," she whispered as he retracted his fangs and licked the small wounds closed.

"You're not going to die, and although there is nothing I want more than to have my hands all over you, I'm not going to. I want your sober consent when I do..." the Doomer whispered in her ear, encircling her waist with his arm and tucking her against his big, strong body.

As he led her outside, she rested her head on his shoulder. Her arm going across his broad back, she delighted in the feel of all those incredible muscles flexing under her roaming palm—dimly aware that they must've looked like a couple in love to the few pedestrians they were passing by.

With her legs too wobbly to support her weight, the Doomer was propping her up and holding her glued to his side. She moved because he wanted her to move: the venom making her uncharacteristically docile and submissive.

Somewhere at the back of her mind, Amanda caught wisps of random, disconnected thoughts.

So that's the real purpose of the venom.

Who needs seduction and foreplay when all a male has to do is grab a female by the neck and bite her for her to welcome him between her thighs...

Who knew it would feel so damn good...

Why is that insufferable man refusing to touch me?

I'm so wet...

Is he going to kill me?
He said he wouldn't.
Didn't he?

24

DALHU

As they walked the few blocks from the jewelry store to the restaurant where he'd left his car, Dalhu was counting the seconds. He wanted to take her as far away as he could, as fast as he could, fearing that any moment someone would come running to her rescue. Someone like a Guardian… or two…

And the scent of her arousal wasn't helping either. He was so painfully stiff, he could barely walk. When they finally reached his car, he stifled a relieved breath.

They were alone in the parking lot behind the restaurant; nevertheless, Dalhu was glad Amanda was still too woozy to resist him as he helped her inside and buckled her seatbelt, or when he pulled out a pair of handcuffs from the glove compartment and secured them around her wrists. Using a second pair, he closed one cuff on the chain connecting her shackled wrists and attached the other one to the door handle. That way, once her lucidity returned, she wouldn't be able to grab the steering wheel or jump out from the speeding car.

"Kinky…" she purred, squirming in her seat.

"No, sweetheart, just careful and prepared." Dalhu chuckled, shaking his head.

The poor girl will be mortified once she sobers up and remembers her wanton behavior.

He'd have to explain that it had been the venom's fault, not hers. How else would she know? It must've been her first bite.

Pulling out of the parking lot, Dalhu debated what to do next. First priority was to get his other watches from the mansion so he could sell them for some cash. There was no way around it. They'd need lots of money on the run, and using his credit cards or hers was not an option.

But she couldn't be seen by his men because then he'd have to kill them all, and that would look even more suspicious than him just disappearing without a trace.

It would be better if they assumed he had an unlucky encounter with Guardians and was taken out.

Actually, he realized, that would be the perfect cover-up.

25

SYSSI

"*Y*ou look a little flushed, is everything okay?" Andrew cast Syssi a measuring look.

She brought her palm to her forehead. Ever since Andrew's embarrassing questioning session with Amanda, her face had remained warm, but she'd thought nothing of it. Except, it was getting worse. *Damn, why now?* "I feel a little feverish. I'm probably coming down with something, and it couldn't have come at a worse time."

"Why? What's special about today?"

"Kian made a reservation at a very fancy and exclusive restaurant. I was really looking forward to spending a romantic evening with him, and even went to all this trouble to look nice." Syssi pointed at her face and shook her head to show off her new hairdo. Then lifted her hands and wiggled her fingers, showing him her manicure.

"Yes, I was wondering why you look different today. I thought it must be love…" he teased.

"That too…"

"Seriously? You're in love with the guy? You just met him, for Pete's sake…"

"I know, but I can't help the way I feel. I love Kian…"

"Kian who? Now, I really need to do a thorough background check on him."

"I don't know." Syssi felt stupid. She'd never bothered to ask.

"You claim to love the guy, and you don't even know his last name…" Andrew shook his head, his expression disapproving.

"I assumed it was the same as Amanda's, but later I found out they had different fathers. So I'm not sure anymore, okay? It's not such a big deal. I'll ask him tonight. And no… I'm not going to tell you so you can dig into his background. You can forget about it." Syssi crossed her arms over her chest, ready to butt heads with her stubborn brother. God only knew what Andrew could discover if he were to snoop into Kian's business.

Surprising her, he just smiled. "As you wish… Don't come crying to me, though, when later you discover things you wish you'd known before; previous marriages, illegitimate kids, prior incarcerations… Small things like that…"

"Oh, just drop it, Andrew, there is nothing like that lurking in his past." *His very, very long past…*

"Okay, okay…" Andrew raised his palms in mock surrender. "You know I'm doing it out of love. Someone has to look after you. You're just too nice and trusting."

"I love you too, Andrew. But I'm a big girl now, and you need to start trusting my judgment. You cannot protect me from everything and everyone at all times. I can take care of myself…" Syssi was starting to feel even worse. Forcing a weak smile, she said, "I think I'd better go. I feel really crappy." Trying to get up, she got dizzy and had to grab the back of her chair to steady herself.

"I'll walk you to the car." Andrew wrapped his arm around her so she could lean on him as they made their way to the limo waiting for her in the back.

"A limousine… Nice… Now, I'm really curious," Andrew taunted.

With no energy to keep it up, she didn't respond. Casting her a worried look, Andrew dropped it. Still, she had no doubt he'd go snooping around— regardless of her asking him not to.

Pulling her into his arms, Andrew kissed the top of her head, then helped her inside. "Take care of yourself, and call me if you need anything. You hear?"

"I will. It's probably nothing."

26

DALHU

*I*t took Dalhu about ten minutes to find a motel. As he stopped and got them a room, he couldn't care less that it seemed questionable. With Amanda already looking a lot less dazed, he was running out of time.

With a quick glance, he made sure there was no one in the parking lot before he uncuffed her, scooped her up in his arms and carried her inside. Kicking the door closed behind him, he didn't waste any time before gently laying her out on the bed and securing her wrists to the slatted wooden headboard.

"Ohh, I feel like a bride on a bondage honeymoon…" she giggled and swiveled her hips in invitation.

Taking a moment to look her over, he was struck again by how beautiful she was. "You're magnificent…" He rubbed his mouth with his hand, wanting her so badly, it hurt. But he couldn't have her, not yet, because sure as hell, she was still very much high on his venom.

Amanda didn't appreciate his efforts one bit. "Would you put us both out of our misery and fuck me already? Is this your idea of torture? You're such a jerk! I'm going insane with lust, and with my hands cuffed like this I can't even do anything about it myself…" she hissed at him, stunning him speechless.

Apparently, he had a lot to learn about immortal females, or maybe just this one. Defying his expectations, instead of cussing him out for abducting her, she was mad because he refused to have sex with her...

Go figure...

Sitting beside her on the bed, he was careful not to touch her as he looked into her eyes, checking for the glazed look he was expecting to find. Amanda's eyes seemed clearer, though her pinched expression made it obvious that she was suffering for real. Evidently, there was another thing he hadn't known about immortal females—their needs were just as over-powering as the males'.

Dalhu sighed. "I have to go and get us some money, but I'll give you something to make you sleep, making it easier for you until the venom leaves your system. And if you still feel the same when you wake up... then I promise, I'll take care of you..." Gently, almost reverently, he touched his palm to her cheek and caressed it lightly. "I'll always take care of you..."

"What do you want from me?" she whispered.

"A future..." He sighed again. "A life partner, a family, everything..." Gazing at her stunned expression, he held his palm to her cheek for a moment longer. "I know you don't want this with me right now. But I promise I'll do everything I can to earn your love. You shall want for nothing..."

Dalhu pushed off the bed, walked over to the dresser, and took one of the motel's two complimentary water bottles. Reaching into his pocket, he pulled out a plastic packet and emptied its powdery contents into the water, then shook the bottle lightly.

"Drink!" He touched the bottle to her lips. "It'll only make you sleep, nothing else."

Amanda pressed her lips tightly closed and shook her head from side to side.

"We can do it the easy way, with you being a good girl and drinking it all up, or the hard way, with me pinching your nose and forcing it down your throat. Your choice." Dalhu didn't want to scare her again, but he didn't have the time or the patience to play games, which, unfortunately, made him sound harsh.

When she opened her mouth to drink, the fear in her eyes as she looked up at him was something he hoped never to see again.

Dalhu tried to be as gentle as he possibly could, supporting her head and making sure she had time to swallow before he gave her more. But in the end, he had her drink it all.

"Good girl," he praised, caressing her cheek as he waited for the drug to do its thing.

"I don't even know your name," she mumbled.

"Dalhu," he told her before her lids fluttered down over her eyes.

27

KIAN

"Master, I'm sorry to bother you, but I think you should come up. Mistress Syssi just returned from her excursion and asked me if we have any Advil. She said she is not feeling well and is going to lie down. I called the front desk and they are sending someone up with the medication, but I thought you would want to know."

"I'm on my way, Okidu." Kian ended the call and rushed to the elevator. *It's probably nothing.* A mortal coming down with a cold or the flu wasn't something to worry about… or was it?

As he entered his bedroom, he found Syssi in bed, shivering, looking flushed and sweaty, the down comforter pulled all the way up to her chin.

"What's wrong, sweetheart?" He sat down beside her and brushed sweaty strands of hair away from her forehead.

"I'm so sorry…" She sniffled, a tear running down her flushed cheek.

"Whatever for?"

"For ruining our plans… I got all pretty for tonight… and now I'm sick… I never get sick… why today?" she whined, looking miserable. "I hate it… I hate feeling weak and useless like this… Did you bring me the Advil?" She wiped a shaky hand across her tear-stained face.

"It will be here in a moment, but I think we need to get Bridget to take a look at you before self-medicating." Heading to the bathroom, Kian texted the doctor on the way, then got two wet washcloths to clean Syssi's face with.

After wiping off her smeared makeup, he grabbed a clean one and patted her face to cool it down. "Don't worry about a silly thing like us going out. We'll do it some other night. Just concentrate on getting better. Something tells me you're going to be a very fussy patient." He forced a smile in an attempt to cheer her up.

"I know, right? Who gets all teary-eyed over a little fever?" She smiled a little smile and took a shaky breath.

"Master, Dr. Bridget is here." Okidu let the doctor in. "And I also have the Advil Mistress Syssi requested, and a glass of water for her to wash it down with." He placed the items on the side table.

"May I trade places with you, Kian?" Bridget motioned for the bed, dropping her doctor's bag on the side table next to the Advil.

"So, what exactly is going on?" Bridget asked as she wrapped the blood pressure cuff around Syssi's bicep.

"I feel crappy. I'm cold and sweaty at the same time. I think I have a fever."

"Any aches and pains? Sore throat? Runny nose?" Bridget removed the cuff and touched the thermometer to Syssi's ear.

"I feel weak and my bones hurt... can bones hurt? No sore throat, though, and no runny nose... I'm sniffling because I've been crying...," Syssi said in a small voice, dropping her eyes to look down at her hands.

"Well, your blood pressure is a little high, and your temperature is a hundred and one. It's elevated, but not dangerous. Let me take a blood sample as well." She pulled a syringe and a packet of antiseptic gauze from her bag.

"Any nausea? Stomach cramps?" she asked as she took Syssi's blood, quickly and efficiently.

Syssi didn't even cringe. "No, just general discomfort."

"Well, that rules out food poisoning," Bridget mumbled, returning the tools of her trade to her bag.

"So what do you think?" Kian stuffed his hands in his back pockets, forcing himself to stay put and not pace like a caged animal.

"I think we should bring Syssi down to my clinic. I want to hook her up to the monitors. I'll send one of the guys with a gurney." Bridget pushed up from the bed and lifted her doctor's bag off the bedside table. Standing, she looked first at Kian, then at Syssi. "I'll know more when I take a look at your blood, Syssi. For now, it doesn't look like a cold or the flu, or food poisoning… It might be some other viral or bacterial infection… Or it might be the start of the change." Bridget dropped the bomb.

28

DALHU

Dalhu made the drive from the motel to the mansion in exactly eight minutes, and left the car idling in front of the entry as he rushed in and up the stairs. Taking them two at a time, he ignored the men greeting him as he passed them by on the way to his room.

Once there, he opened the safe and emptied its contents into a duffle bag. There wasn't much, just his two other watches and what remained of the money he was entrusted with for the mission's cash expenses.

His weapons were in a fireproof lockbox in the master walk-in closet. Crouching over the open lid, he pulled out the semi and the nine-millimeter handgun, loaded them, and then double checked the safety before screwing the silencer on the SIG.

The knives were next.

Dalhu strapped two of them to his biceps and one on his calf, and four more went into the duffle bag. Whatever space was left, he filled with boxes of ammunition. Zipping the bag closed, he slung it over his shoulder, then grabbed a jacket on his way out.

Taking a look around the master bedroom, he scanned for anything else he might need. His laptop was on the nightstand, next to the picture of his beautiful woman. He took both, reshuffling the contents of the bag to make room.

The last items he decided to add didn't require a lot of space. Opening his desk drawer, Dalhu took out a bunch of plastic packets and shoved them into the side pocket of the duffle bag. Who knew how many more times he'd have to drug his beauty to sleep?

And besides, they might prove useful in other situations. He needed all the resources he could put his hands on.

As he slipped on his jacket over his personal arsenal, Dalhu quickly decided on a probable cover story to tell his men—one that would explain his rush and buy him some time.

On his way out, he grabbed the first man on his path. "I've identified an enemy male entering a restaurant less than one mile away from here. A Guardian. I came back for my weapons." Dalhu clapped the man's shoulder before dashing down the stairs.

"Need backup, commander?" the man called after his retreating back.

"No, the fucker is mine." Dalhu slammed the door behind him and ran the short distance to his car.

29

KIAN

"Have you ever witnessed a transition start like this?" Kian's voice faltered as dread squeezed his heart like a vise.

"It's rare, but there were instances where a transitioning boy, in addition to the normal pains of growing venom glands and fangs, developed a fever accompanied by skeletal pains. So it's a definite possibility, although all the girls transition smoothly with no side effects."

"Is there anything we can do?" Kian ran a shaky hand through his hair.

"Unfortunately, there is nothing that can be done other than waiting. That's why I want Syssi monitored. I have no idea how severely the transition could affect an adult female." Bridget gave them an apologetic look. "I'll send the gurney up."

Kian sat back on the bed and took Syssi in his arms. "I love you so much," he said, hating how desperate he sounded.

"Why are you so sad? This is exactly what we were hoping for," Syssi whispered, trying to return his embrace. But holding her arms up proved to be too much of an exertion in her weakened state and she let them drop.

Kian sighed. "I'm scared shitless. Not knowing what's going on and powerless to do anything to make it better for you is driving me insane." His body sagged in defeat.

"Don't. I need you to stay strong for both of us," Syssi whispered. "Can you hand me that water?"

"Of course, my love." He brought the glass to her lips, propping her head with his hand as she drank.

A knock on the open door was followed by Anandur and Brundar's worry-lined faces peeking in. "We brought the gurney. How is Syssi?" Anandur asked.

"Not so good, you can leave the gurney out in the hallway. I'll carry her out." Kian pushed up from the bed and walked over to close the door. "Thank you, guys. I'll keep you informed..."

As he turned around and faced Syssi, Kian squared his shoulders and plastered a smile on his face. "Would you like to change into a nightshirt before I take you to the clinic?" He peeled the comforter off her.

"Can you help me shower first? I'm sweaty and sticky." Syssi was shaking so hard that her teeth chattered.

Kian felt like crying. But Syssi was right, he had to man up and be strong for both of them. She needed him to take care of her and not fall apart like a wimp...

What the hell was wrong with him anyway?

When did he become so weak?

"Sure, let me prepare a bath for you, I'll be right back."

To keep her warm, Kian pulled the comforter back up to Syssi's chin, then hurried to the bathroom and cranked the thermostat all the way up before running hot water for her bath.

30

DALHU

Finding Amanda still fast asleep when he returned, Dalhu sighed in relief. The drug was supposed to keep a mortal out for a couple of hours. But even though the whole round-trip took him less than half that, which should've left him with plenty of time to spare, this kind of thing wasn't a precise science.

And more to the point—his captive wasn't mortal.

He still couldn't believe how lucky he was. He had done the impossible, snagging himself an immortal female, and not just any immortal, but the stunning professor. Now that he had her, he would do everything in his power to keep her, and the last thing he needed was her waking up and sounding the alarm.

On the way back, he'd gotten rid of her cell phone, smashing and dumping it in a big trash bin next to a strip mall he'd passed. And he'd done the same with his own for good measure, despite it being the prepaid kind. It was vital for both of them to disappear from the grid.

If captured, he was a dead man, regardless of who found them first, her clansmen or his fellow Doomers. He had to find them some deserted place —somewhere far and secluded so his captive would have nowhere to run… and no one to hear her cries for help. After all, he couldn't keep her drugged and chained to a bed. That would certainly not endear him to her. He needed a safe place where he would have at least a shadow of a chance to win her heart.

His best option was to find a remote cabin—a winter retreat unoccupied during the summer months. Before going there, he would need to gather supplies to last them a couple of weeks. Hopefully, by the time they ran out and needed to go for more, she'd warm to him, and he'd figure out what to do next.

Dalhu pulled out his laptop and typed in the motel's Wi-Fi password, connecting to the Internet, then opened Google Maps and started his search.

Let's find us a nice place to hide.

31

KIAN

Kian pulled out a chair and sat next to Syssi's bed in the clinic, holding her limp hand as he listened to the rhythmic sound of her heart monitor. Covered in the warmed blankets Bridget had supplied, she had thankfully stopped shivering and had fallen asleep.

He heard Bridget's light footsteps coming up behind him. "I have Syssi's blood results," she said quietly.

"And?"

"I'm still not sure what's going on. It's definitely not a bacterial infection, and I'm pretty sure it's not viral. My best guess is that she is going through the transition."

"Be honest with me, is she in danger?" Kian pinned Bridget with an uncompromising stare.

"I honestly don't know. Her heart is doing all right, and the fever is not high enough to be dangerous, and it's holding steady. But her blood pressure is climbing."

Kian shook his head. "I feel so helpless, wishing there was something I could do. I have no idea how mortals deal with things like that, watching their loved ones get sick, not knowing if they'll pull through. Their existence is so short and full of misery."

Mortality.

Kian was no stranger to death claiming loved ones. He had watched generations of his descendants live their lives and die. But most managed to live to an old age, in no small part thanks to his discreet help. And he had been away when his brother Lilen had fallen, finding out about the tragedy only after the fact. But never before had he felt as helpless and useless as he was feeling now. With all of his clan resources—the money, the advanced technology—he was forced to watch, powerless, as the woman he loved fought for her life.

Bridget patted his shoulder. "They deal because they have to. If it would help, you might try praying. Mortals find it calming and reassuring at times like this."

32

AMANDA

*A*manda woke up with her arms stiff from being pulled over her head. Still groggy, she had a moment of confusion trying to figure out why she couldn't bring them down.

Dalhu, the name popped into her waking mind—the lunatic Doomer who wanted to make her his wife. Concentrating, she tried to remember everything he had said and done so she could figure a way out of this mess. Taking a peek from under her lashes, she looked around the dingy motel room, finding him hunched over a laptop.

First thing first, however, she needed out of these handcuffs. Her arms hurt too much to think clearly.

"Hey you, Dalhu, how about removing these cuffs. My arms hurt."

Startled, he jumped. "You're awake." Dalhu walked over and unfastened the cuffs, then sat down beside her on the bed and began massaging her stiff muscles.

Amanda said nothing, watching the Doomer as he worked at her kinks with surprisingly gentle hands. He was quite handsome: dark short hair, dark big eyes, and a classically structured face. Not to mention a big, powerful, yummy body...

It was such a shame that he was broken...

"What are you planning to do with me?" she asked.

Looking at her as if she were a hard-won prize, Dalhu kept massaging and bringing circulation back to her arms. Then, when she thought he wouldn't answer her, he took hold of her hand and brought it to his lips for a kiss. "We are going to run—away from your people and mine. I found us a place to hide for a while. We will get to know each other... get close..."

His eyes were so full of hope that she felt sorry for the delusional bastard. "A modern time Romeo and Juliet running away from their families, with just one small twist: Juliet doesn't want to run, she is happy where she is..."

"Are you happy, Professor? With no mate? And no hope of ever finding one? Just going through your life alone? I know I wasn't happy. I just existed, not really living through the long centuries of my life until I found you and grabbed a chance. We are each other's only hope. Face it, there are no other compatible mates for us. It's either this or a very long and lonely life. I'm willing to do whatever it takes to make us happen. How about you give us the same chance?" The besotted look was gone, replaced by iron determination.

Amanda was speechless for a moment. The lunatic actually made sense... or maybe she was just losing it, succumbing to the Stockholm syndrome. "Could you bring me some water, please?" She bought herself a few moments to gather her thoughts.

Sipping slowly from the fresh water bottle he had handed her, she speculated that he'd found out her name and title by going through her purse. Probably had gotten rid of her phone as well, eliminating the only chance of anyone locating her. It was up to her to convince him to let her go...

Yeah, right, as if that is going to work.

Except, with no other options she had to at least try.

Okay, here goes nothing...

"I understand your logic, but it's flawed." Amanda assumed her teacher's voice, preparing for a lecture. The Doomer was crazy but not stupid, maybe she could make him see the light. "We come from very different worlds, different values, different beliefs, opposing beliefs actually, conflicting goals. We are each other's worst enemies. These kinds of differences could never be reconciled, and you cannot build a house on such a shaky foundation, for it will crumble and fall. I'm sorry, but this will never work between us." Amanda actually reached for his hand in an effort to comfort him.

He caressed the back of her hand with his thumb, smiling at her as if she were a misguided fool. "Didn't I tell you I'll do whatever it takes? You want me to take up your clan's humanitarian mission? I'll do it. You want me to forsake the Brotherhood? Already done. I don't give a flying fuck about either. All I want is a little piece of heaven with you, and I'll do whatever it takes to make you happy." He looked triumphant; there was nothing she could say to that.

"It's not that simple," was all she could manage on the spot.

"It is. Unless you can honestly say that you find me repulsive, ugly..." Dalhu arched a brow.

Damn, remembering how she'd begged him to fuck her, she knew she couldn't lie about this. "No, I can't say that... You're not completely unfortunate in the looks department." Amanda shrugged dismissively.

"That's the best you could do? Come on, Professor, I'm sure you have something better up your sleeve." Dalhu lifted her hand up for a kiss, moving his thick, firm lips back and forth over the back of it, sending shivers down her spine.

Did he have to be this sexy? Really? Bad guys were supposed to be ugly and mean. It just wasn't fair. "I'll think of something. I promise." And she meant it. There must be something that would burst his hopeful bubble.

She just had to find what it was.

33

KIAN

"Master Kian, may I bother you for a moment?" Onidu asked from beyond the threshold.

Kian tensed, knowing that Onidu would never disturb him unless it was important. Releasing Syssi's hand, he laid it gently on top of the warming blanket, then stepped out of the room and closed the door quietly behind him. "What's going on, Onidu?"

"It is Mistress Amanda. She is not back yet, and I suspect something is wrong. She told Mistress Syssi that she had a few errands to run, and would call me when she was done or take a taxicab home. But it is already after eight, and Mistress Amanda is not back yet."

"Did you call her? She might have gone to a club or to have dinner somewhere. You know how she is."

"I called, but she did not answer."

"Amanda might be in a noisy place and didn't hear the ring." Kian pulled out his phone and selected Amanda's contact. The call went straight to voice mail.

He started worrying in earnest. It wasn't that Amanda hadn't done this type of thing before, she had, plenty of times. But she usually answered her phone—her immortal hearing sufficient to hear the ring even over a club's deafening noise.

Except, it was entirely possible that she was busy with some guy in a back room, and though it was a bit early for that, it was still the most likely explanation.

Hell, he really didn't need this on top of what was going on with Syssi, but knowing that doubt would keep eating at him till he made sure Amanda was all right, he got Onegus on the line. "We have what might be a situation. Amanda hasn't returned home yet, and she is not answering her phone. Could you send the guys to check her usual hangouts? Better yet, get William to track her phone signal."

"I'm on it, boss." Onegus ended the call.

34

DALHU

*A*fter leaving the motel, Dalhu found a large shopping mall and turned into its underground parking.

"Are you taking me shopping?" Amanda asked as soon as she realized where he was heading. "So nice of you," she mocked.

He glanced her way, a smirk curling his lips. "I promise I will take you shopping later, but not now, and not here."

"Really?" She looked surprised.

"Really." What he had in mind was breaking into some store later at night and grabbing provisions for the mountains. But for now, he'd let her think what she would.

Waiting for the right opportunity to present itself, he slowly drove around the parking garage. Going down a few levels, Dalhu eventually found what he was looking for. A young man was exiting his car, and there was nobody else around. Not wasting any time, Dalhu stopped and got out of his Mercedes.

Thralling the young man to trade his old, battered Honda for Dalhu's rental took only a few seconds. Hopefully, it would take the Brotherhood some time to track the Mercedes to the guy and start looking for the Honda.

Dalhu was taking every precaution he could think of.

Amanda made a face as he rushed her to the passenger seat of the small car. "You are really taking me slumming. At least the Mercedes was something I was comfortable being driven in. This car is just blah, and it smells." Amanda resumed the nonstop complaining she had started as soon as they left the motel, probably hoping he would grow sick of her annoying company and decide she wasn't worth the trouble.

Oh, man, she had it wrong. He couldn't imagine anything that would detract from how much he wanted her. She could've sung for hours, off key, while farting, and he would've found it charming.

"It's not going to work, Professor. I know what you're trying to do." Dalhu smirked.

"Stop calling me Professor. Why do you do that anyway?"

"Because I can't believe how lucky I got. My woman is gorgeous and smart—a professor no less—it makes me proud to say it."

"Well, I don't like it. Call me Amanda. You sound condescending when you say professor."

"How do you figure that?"

"You say it as if I'm stupid despite being well educated."

Dalhu glanced her way before returning his eyes to the road. "Guilty as charged. You are being stupid if you think this constant nagging will change my mind. I just tune it out."

"Insufferable man..." she spat.

35

KIAN

"We checked all of the clubs; she wasn't at any of them. And William couldn't get a signal. He said her phone is history." Onegus delivered the dire news.

Kian was going slowly insane.

Syssi had gone from sleeping to losing consciousness, and now this. Frantic with worry, he paced the small room, feeling like his world was crumbling around him and he was powerless to do a damn thing about it.

Maybe I should pray. Kian's face twisted in a sardonic grimace. *If only I could think of a deity I could pray to...* He stopped in his tracks and pulled out his phone.

"It's Kian, put my mother on the line, please. It's urgent." He resumed his pacing.

"What happened?" Annani came on line, her melodic voice instantly providing him with a measure of relief.

Sighing, he felt like a small boy again, when sharing his troubles with his mother had always managed to make him feel better. "I met a girl, Syssi, and she is a Dormant."

"I know all about her." Kian heard the smile in his mother's voice.

"How?" he asked, awed by her astounding powers.

"Nothing profound, Kian, we do get texts and phone calls up here. The news traveled through the grapevine." She chuckled at his misconception.

"I see… Anyway, Syssi is transitioning and is not doing well. She lost consciousness a little while ago, and we don't know what to do. And to top it off, Amanda is missing." He waited for Annani to say something.

"I am flying over. I will be there in a few hours," she said after a short pause.

Kian was torn between wanting his mother's support and keeping her safely away. "No, Mother, you can't come. It's too dangerous. With the Doomers here in LA, we can't risk your safety like this."

"My daughter is missing, my future daughter-in-law is unconscious, and you think I will stay here twiddling my fingers? I am coming, whether you like it or not. Have the helicopter ready to pick me up from our airstrip." She waited for him to say something. "Kian, this is where you say yes, Mother," she supplied.

"Yes, Mother… but it's thumbs. Not fingers."

"What?"

"The expression is twiddling my thumbs."

3 6

DALHU

"So, now you added stealing to your list of crimes, along with kidnapping." As soon as Dalhu was done loading the car with the last of the supplies, Amanda resumed her incessant nagging.

Driving on a dark and deserted mountain road, he'd found a small shopping center. Closed for the night, with no soul for miles around, the decrepit wooden building housing a general store and a donut shop looked creepily like something one would expect to find in a ghost town. But it was exactly what he'd been looking for.

The simple lock had posed no real challenge for Dalhu, and as he'd suspected, the store had no alarm system.

He'd piled on canned foods, loaves of bread, and drinks. Looking around for more items that were not too difficult to prepare, he'd grabbed several packages of ramen noodles and, some spaghetti, along with canned spaghetti sauce. His own expertise in the cooking department was limited, and he had no illusions as to Amanda's willingness to prepare food for them.

There were a few racks of garments for both men and women at the back of the store, and he'd picked sweats for Amanda and himself. Luckily, he'd found some XXL sweats. They were cheaply made, not to mention too short, but beggars couldn't be choosers. They would have to do.

Despite her loud protests, he'd left Amanda cuffed in the car while he'd gathered the supplies. She'd retaliated by making him go back time and again for towels, blankets, toiletries, and other things she'd figured they would need.

She was right, of course. They had no way of knowing what they would find in the deserted cabin he planned on breaking into, wisely making sure that they would at least have the bare necessities.

So why the hell was she suddenly throwing that in his face when only a few minutes ago she was sending him for more things?

His gaze cut to her. "If that was the sum of my crimes, I would be a happy man," he grated. Then seeing her shrink away from him, he added in a softer tone, "If it makes you feel any better, I left three hundred bucks on the counter to cover what we took. I may be many things, but I'm not a thief."

37

AMANDA

Reminded of who and what her kidnapper was, Amanda's bravado faltered. He was a Doomer, for goodness' sake, by definition a cold-blooded, professional killer. She must've been out of her mind pushing him the way she had. She should tread lightly around him and shut up, instead of antagonizing him.

The smart thing to do was to wait patiently to be rescued. Except, how would anyone find her? Had they even noticed that she was missing? Kian and Syssi were probably still on their date, oblivious to her fate. Only Onidu would know something was wrong. It was sad, really, that the only person waiting for her to come home wasn't really a person.

Stop feeling sorry for yourself.

Kian and Syssi would be worried sick about her just as soon as they found out. And so would be the rest of her family. They'd do everything in their power to get her back.

"Why are you so quiet all of a sudden?" Dalhu studied her face in the dim illumination of the dashboard lights.

"I thought my nagging was annoying you," she said without looking at him.

"Nah, I like the sound of your voice… even with the whiny undertones."

Forgetting her newfound resolve of only a moment ago, she hazarded,

"You sounded like you have regrets, are they for all the killing you have done?"

Stupid! Stupid! Stupid! Why can't I keep my mouth shut?

Dalhu pinned her with an unreadable look before turning his eyes back on the road. "Regrets are for those who had a choice and made the wrong one. I didn't have a choice. So no, I have no regrets. That doesn't mean, however, that I'm happy with the way my life has turned out." Dalhu paused as if deliberating whether to tell her more.

Amanda's silence eventually prompted him to continue. "My mother was a slave and a whore with no say in her life either, and yet she loved me despite the way she came to have me. Which could not have been said for the rest of the women at the harem; some hated the children that were forced upon them. After all this time, even though I can't recall her face anymore, I still remember her crying when I was torn from her arms and taken to be activated and raised as a warrior in a cold and cruel military training camp. That camp and its teachings of hate and war became my whole life, and I never saw her or my sister again. I could feel sorry for myself and indulge in wishing that my life's circumstances were different, but that's all it would be—wishing. It would change nothing."

Chewing on her lower lip, Amanda reflected on what he'd told her. He was right. She grew up pampered and sheltered, never having to face the things he had since he'd been a young boy. Could she blame him? Judge him? Not really. But the fact remained that after a lifetime of hatred and killing, Dalhu was no doubt broken beyond repair, and to think differently would be wishful and naive. It was exactly as he had said; wishing would not make it so.

Glancing at his hard profile, Amanda felt a mixture of pity and grudging respect for him. Somehow, through all that he'd done and all that had been done to him, he'd managed to keep a tiny bit of himself out of the darkness, and with that flickering flame, he still hoped and struggled to feel something other than hatred and rage. It made her curious. The scientist in her hankered to discover how he was able to do it after centuries of living in what must have been a damn close approximation of hell.

"So what now? Did you really leave the Brotherhood just for me, or did something change?"

Dalhu didn't respond right away. Staring at the dark, winding road ahead, he tightened his grip on the steering wheel. "A lot has changed. I'm almost eight hundred years old, Amanda. I got tired of the fighting and the killing... and I learned. This new era of easily accessible information opened my eyes and made me realize that we were being brainwashed and lied to; pretty much about everything. From the moment I figured it out, I began planning an exit strategy and buying this ridiculously expensive jewelry so I would have something to trade for money when the time was right..." He lifted his hand off the steering wheel, showing her his Rolex and his ring. "When I saw you, I knew I'd never have another chance like that. It was time to take the plunge and run. And here we are..." He smiled and patted her knee.

"That's nice, Dalhu, but what happens when the money runs out? What then?"

"I'll worry about it when the time comes. There is always a market for my kind of skills. I'll find something. Don't worry, I'll take care of you." Dalhu squeezed her knee reassuringly.

"I bet you will." Amanda could just imagine the type of skills he'd been referring to. "I guess you're not talking about becoming a lumberjack, or a professional wrestler." She chuckled with a sidelong glance at him.

"If that's what turns you on, why not? But for some reason, I can't imagine a woman like you managing on a lumberjack's pay or coming to cheer me on at a wrestling match..." He gave her outfit an appreciative look-over. "Even I know that what you're wearing must have cost thousands."

"Seeing you shirtless and covered in sweat might be worth the slumming..." Amanda just couldn't help herself. She was used to saying whatever was on her mind, and once the image had formed, she hadn't stopped to think before blurting it out.

"Happy to oblige, ma'am. I'll gladly take my shirt off right now." He chuckled. "If that's all it takes to turn you on, I'm a lucky, lucky man."

"Nah, it's too cold for sweating, and it's not the same without." Amanda shrugged, her lips twitching in an effort to suppress the urge to smile.

"I can think of a surefire way you can make me sweat... you can take *your* shirt off." Dalhu regarded her with a leering grin.

38

DALHU

Dalhu was enjoying the lighthearted banter they had going on. He'd never experienced that with a woman before, and besides providing a pleasant respite from the shit-scape of his mind, it was turning him on.

Tonight, he hoped she'd let him take care of her the way she had begged him to do before. She might need a little coaxing, but he had a feeling it wouldn't take much to seduce her. Amanda was forward and lustful, and she'd already admitted that she found him attractive.

Testing, he slowly moved his hand across her knee to caress the inside of her thigh. Her sharp inhale was muffled.

Dalhu smirked. She shouldn't have bothered to hide her reaction. She forgot that he could smell the spike in her arousal.

Well, what do you know? He had been right. Dalhu smiled and returned his hand to her knee.

Distracted by carnal thoughts, he almost missed the turn onto the dirt road leading up to the secluded cabin. As he slammed on the brakes, the car swerved as he made a sharp turn, skidding on the loose gravel before coming to a full stop.

"Nice driving," Amanda grated.

He shrugged and got out.

The rusted lock securing the simple metal gate at the bottom of the hill required only minimal manipulation to open, and he relocked it behind them before driving up the heavily wooded mountain trail.

It was a little past midnight when he finally parked the car at the end of the long, private driveway.

The place was perfect, just as he had known it would be from the close-up Google image he had pulled up at the motel. With no other dwellings for miles around and no power lines leading up to it, the cabin was completely off the grid. A solar array and a decent-sized wind turbine provided its power. And a water well equipped with an electrical pump took care of the water supply.

The chances of anyone being able to track them to this remote, isolated location were slim to none, as were Amanda's opportunities to run or get help.

Flipping the light switch on, Dalhu was relieved to find that the power was working just fine. He took an appraising look at the cabin's plain interior. The downstairs was one big room, with a simple L-shaped kitchen and a narrow wooden staircase leading up to an open loft-style bedroom. Both rooms were sparsely furnished with old, well-worn pieces that were currently covered with a thick layer of dust.

A massive brick fireplace, flanked by windows going all the way up to the gabled ceiling, was the cabin's one redeeming grace. He liked the simple, homey feel, but he had to admit that it was definitely not up to his woman's standards.

With a grimace that conveyed her opinion louder than words, Amanda clutched her purse close to her body as if to prevent it from touching the grime. "I'm going to pee and take a bath. You go ahead and start cleaning. This place is filthy." Without sparing him a second look, she took the stairs up to the loft and strode into the cabin's only bathroom, locking the door behind her.

"Pampered brat," Dalhu mumbled under his breath.

"I heard that!" she said, flushing the toilet.

"Good!" He answered loudly this time, following her up the rickety stairs and dropping the bags he had carried up on the dusty bed cover. In need of the facilities himself, he waited for her to get out.

But then, a squeak of an old faucet, followed by the sound of water hitting the bottom of a tub, made him realize that the selfish woman had started a bath without considering that he might need to use the bathroom as well.

No big deal; he could take care of business outside.

Once that most pressing need was satisfied, Dalhu finished unloading the Honda and drove it off the driveway, hiding it in the thicket. He made sure it was well covered with heavy greenery, in case someone thought to do an aerial search for the missing car. The keys went under the floorboards of the porch, safely hidden, and out of Amanda's reach.

Back in the cabin, Dalhu took a calculating look at the thick layer of dust covering every exposed surface and the spider webs hanging from ceiling corners and between furniture legs. No matter how dirty the place was, it was small enough for him to have it cleaned before the spoiled princess finished taking her bath. And hopefully, by the time he was done, he would manage to work up a little sweat...

Imagining Amanda's lustful response to his half-naked, glistening body, he felt a surge of arousal. Now that he knew her weakness, he planned to exploit it.

"Game on, Professor." With a wicked smile tugging at the corner of his mouth, Dalhu took off his shirt and went to work.

39

KIAN

Outside Syssi's room, Kian found most of the Guardians keeping vigil, sitting or sprawling on the hallway's thinly carpeted floor. The only two absent were on their way to escort his mother when she arrived.

"Any news?" he asked Onegus.

"William is still working on hacking every relevant security camera in the area that's connected to the web. He even mobilized his geek squad to help."

"His geek squad?"

"You know, the class he's teaching. You should see it, it's like a fucking war room down in his lair."

"What about the police; did you talk to the chief?"

"Yeah, I impressed upon him that our continued contributions are contingent upon the level of attention he's going to dedicate to this case. Every cop in the state has Amanda's picture by now and is searching for any possible clues. Someone must've seen something, it's not like she could've disappeared into thin air or went unnoticed. Amanda doesn't exactly blend in."

"That's why I'm so worried. She could disappear into thin air if someone thralled everyone who had seen her getting nabbed. If the Doomers got her..." Kian couldn't finish his sentence. The horrific implications of that eventuality were just too much for him to bear.

He knew he was starting to crack, the fissures becoming longer and deeper with every passing hour without a shred of good news on either front. He held on because he had to; because there was no one else to shoulder the responsibility and relieve him of his burden.

It was absurd, but Kian had the feeling that the moment his mother arrived, he would just let go and shatter to pieces.

And how fucking pathetic was that?

40

AMANDA

The racket Amanda heard coming from beyond the bathroom door sounded as if Dalhu was tearing the place apart instead of cleaning it up.

She heard him hauling the mattress outside and then beating the hell out of it with what sounded like a bat. Wincing, she imagined the clouds of dust that were billowing out of the old, dirty thing. Then came the sound of the noisy, cheap vacuum going on and on as Dalhu battled the dust on the rest of the stuff.

Soaking in the bathtub that she'd had to clean with her own two hands, Amanda had to admit Dalhu had been right to call her a spoiled, pampered brat. This was the first time she had done anything even remotely domestic. Ever. Unfortunately, there had been no way around it if she wanted to use the deep, but dirty claw-foot tub.

Now, as the water was cooling, she also realized she'd forgotten to bring in the toiletries and a towel. At her home, Onidu was the one who made sure they were on hand for her. She never had to bother with something so trivial herself.

She was stuck.

Okay... her options were to either run out naked and dripping or call Dalhu for help. Both sucked.

She was about to make a run for it, when the vacuum's incessant drone stopped, replaced by the sound of Dalhu's heavy footfalls going up the creaking wooden steps.

Forcing the door open, he walked right in. "Hello, princess." He grinned like the cat who was about to swallow Tweety Bird.

When she didn't gasp or try to cover herself as most women would, the surprised look on his face was priceless. But why would she? She was nothing like what he was used to.

Not even close.

Amanda was the daughter of a goddess, for fate's sake.

Her naked body, boldly displayed in the bath's clear water, rendered Dalhu speechless and drooling. He wasn't the only one affected, though. As he devoured her with his hungry eyes, her body responded, her small nipples growing taut under his hooded gaze.

Wiping the drool off his mouth with the back of his dirty hand, Dalhu ogled her, looking just as awestruck as one of her students. But that was where the resemblance ended.

Dalhu was a magnificent specimen of manhood, and in comparison, all her prior partners were mere boys. Shirtless and sweaty, he looked just as amazing as she had imagined he would.

He was big, not even Yamanu was that tall, and Dalhu was more powerfully built. Nevertheless, his well-defined muscles were perfectly proportioned for his size with no excess bulk; he looked strong, but not pumped like someone who spent endless hours lifting weights at a gym.

Following the light smattering of dark hair trailing down the center of his chest to where it disappeared below the belt line of his jeans, she wasn't surprised to find that he was well proportioned everywhere. And as he kept staring at her, mesmerized, his jeans growing too tight to contain him, she held her breath in anticipation of her first glimpse of that magnificent shaft poking above his belt.

Oh, boy, am I in a shitload of trouble.

There was just no way she could resist all that yummy maleness. Amanda knew she was going to succumb to temptation.

She always had.

Except, this time, she would be stooping lower than ever. Because she could think of nothing that would scream *slut* louder than her going willingly into the arms of her clan's mortal enemy…

41

KIAN

*A*nnani arrived.

In addition to the goddess, the large helicopter landing on the stronghold's rooftop carried her two servants, Oridu and Ogidu, and the two Guardians Kian had dispatched to pick her up from the clan's private airstrip.

Kri exited first, bending her head under the chopper's rotating blades, and offered her hand to help the small, black-robed figure down and away from harm's way.

Kian rushed forward to embrace his mother's slight form, shielding her with his large body from the whirlwind created by the helicopter's slowing blades.

The great, formidable Annani was so tiny and light, he'd been afraid she might get blown away.

Once inside the rooftop vestibule, he let go of her and went down to one knee, kneeling so he wouldn't tower over her.

Annani pulled back her hood, the mass of her red, wavy hair spilling forward and cutting some of the lambent light cast by her luminescent, pale face.

Looking at Kian with eyes full of mother's love, she clasped his scruffy cheeks in her warm palms and bent slightly to kiss his forehead. "I have not seen you in such a long time, I forgot how handsome you are, my beautiful boy."

Ignoring her shameless effort to lay a guilt trip on him, Kian sighed with relief; her tender touch and the sound of her soothing, melodic voice were a salve on the growing fissures of his psyche. "I've missed you too, Mother. I should have visited more often. I allowed myself to get distracted by all things mundane, forgetting what's really important in this miserable life. Forgive me." He hung his head, the truth of his words adding to his despondent mood.

His whole life was work. He neglected his relationships with his sisters and mother, got angry when other family members dared to disturb him, and for what? So he could spend more endless hours bent over reports and contracts? It all felt so meaningless now as his world was falling apart.

"Get up, Kian, and stop that self-flagellation you have got going on. I raised you to be a strong and capable leader. You cannot allow yourself to wallow in self-pity when fate challenges you. Let us go and help your girl pull through." Annani patted his cheek and waited for him to rise.

As he got to his feet and looked down at his tiny but formidable mother, Kian had to smile. She was the strongest, most willful person he knew. Letting nothing bring her down, she relentlessly pushed forward when others would have given up.

Later, in Syssi's room at the clinic, Annani removed her heavy robe and handed it to Kian, then sat on the hospital bed next to Syssi.

Her long, sleeveless, black silk dress was plain, but it clung to her body in a way that made the lack of a bra quite conspicuous. She never wore one. And though his sisters had tried to convince her it was unseemly, she had retorted that as gravity had no effect on her never-aging body, she saw no reason to bother with something so uncomfortable in deference to the transient sensibilities of others. Why should she? After all, she was the goddess, and it was everyone else's duty to show deference to her. Not the other way around.

And who could argue with that?

"She is so lovely," Annani said quietly, running her fingers through Syssi's thick, multicolored hair.

"On the inside as well." Standing next to his mother, Kian was tormented by gut-wrenching worry.

Taking Syssi's hand and holding it between both of hers, his mother asked, "Does she feel as strongly for you as you feel for her?"

"She does."

"And if she pulls through the change, do you plan to mate her for life?"

"Yes, I've never felt like this about anyone. I thought I loved Lavena, but I'm not sure anymore. I know it seems improbable and maybe even foolish for me to feel this way about a woman I've known for such a short time. But I've known Syssi was the one from the first moment I laid eyes on her. Since then, all I've done is prove to myself that my initial gut response was right. I've yet to find even one thing that I don't like about her. I love everything. Even the little snoring sounds she makes when she sleeps—they soothe me." He chuckled, but then his smile wilted, and he rubbed the place over his heart.

"I get crazy jealous and possessive over Syssi, I never did with Lavena. I don't know why... she never does anything to encourage these feelings. It's just me, acting like a caveman who's guarding his turf, all primal instinct and no brains." Glancing at his mother's satisfied smirk, Kian raked his fingers through his hair.

"You react this way because your immortal body and your soul recognize the one woman who completes you, and you would do just about anything to guard her and keep her safely to yourself. It is as it should be for a male of our kind. I am so happy that against all odds, fate—with a little help from Amanda—has granted you this rare fortune of a truelove match... But are you sure Syssi feels the same way about you?"

"Yes, why do you keep asking? Do you have a reason to doubt it?" It was disconcerting the way his mother double checked. Did she think he was not lovable? Or worse, that Syssi was some kind of opportunist? Seeking to gain something other than his love and devotion?

"Close the door, Kian." Annani gestured toward the open door, where the Guardians keeping vigil in the corridor outside were listening in on their conversation.

He had completely forgotten that they were not alone. Now everyone would know how out of control he was.

Whatever… let them.

As he felt a soundproofing shield snap into place, Kian figured his mother wished to guard their conversation. Couldn't she have done it before asking him all those personal questions? Annani was the only one whose power was strong enough to block other immortals, affecting them as easily as they affected humans.

"I kept asking to make sure I was not bringing you in on my most guarded secret without a very good cause." She sighed, gesturing for him to take a seat on the chair beside the bed.

"What I am going to reveal, I shared out of necessity only with Alena. And now I am sharing it with you… The way we turn our girls is not the way we led everyone to believe we do. They cannot turn just by being exposed to my magnificent self." She smiled sheepishly as she paused for effect. "I give them a small infusion of my blood to facilitate the change."

Kian was speechless for a moment. "No wonder you kept it secret. I assume only your blood works? Obviously, if anybody else's had, it wouldn't have been such a big deal."

"Now you understand why I cannot risk it leaking out. I would become even more of a target than I already am. This information must not fall into the wrong hands by someone blurting it accidentally, or it being tortured out of them."

"Yes, you were right to keep it a secret. So how does it work? Was it always done like that with the girls?"

"No, it was not needed when there were enough boys from different matrilineal descent to facilitate the change. The girls were turned at around the same age as the boys, at puberty. It was such a lovely ceremony, similar to an engagement party but not as binding. The girl's family would choose an older transitioned boy, or her future intended if there was one, and throw a big party with lots of food and entertainment. Scantily clothed dancers would put on a show to arouse their audience with their erotic and enticing moves. And at the end of it, the young couple would be escorted to a secluded room for the girl's first kiss and her first bite. Nothing more was allowed, and knowing the consequences, no boy ever crossed the line. A paid substitute was provided for him if later his need became too pressing. And it wasn't because premarital sex was allowed for the boys and not for the girls or any such nonsense; it was just discouraged for those not yet seventeen. In most cases, one bite was enough, but occasionally the boy was called for a repeat performance." With a wistful smile on her lovely face, Annani gazed blankly at the wall.

"So how did you come up with the idea of giving them your blood? Was it ever done before?"

"No. Desperate times called for desperate measures, and I was desperate. We could not use our boys to turn the girls; it would have been considered incest, and as far as we knew, it would carry disastrous consequences. I remembered my uncle mentioning that even a small amount of a god's blood could bring miraculous healing to a mortal, and I figured it was worth a try. The first Dormant girl child was born, of course, to Alena, so obviously I had to ask her permission before trying something potentially dangerous on her daughter. She agreed that we had to try; otherwise, we would've been doomed to extinction and her female children to mortality. Luckily, by the time her first son was born, you were old enough to be his initiator. And the rest is history. We decided to keep it to ourselves, and concocted the story of my amazing ability to bring about the change by my godly presence alone. Truthfully, I did not think anyone would buy it, but they did." Annani shrugged her bare shoulders.

"That's the real reason you came." Kian stated the obvious.

"I would have come regardless, but yes. Your girl should have been fine with your venom alone, but she is not. I figured I could increase her chances of survival by giving her a boost with a tiny infusion of my blood. If she makes it... when she makes it... Syssi could become the mother of a new line, and her descendants could mate with mine. There will be no more need for my blood. She is the key to our future, Kian. I am happy you love her and she loves you back, but I think I would have done it even if that was not the case. She is just too important."

Kian nodded. "Do you know what to do? I'm not good with needles."

"Do not worry about it, by now I am an expert, and I have everything I need with me. Hand me my robe and go stand guard outside. I do not want Bridget catching us in the act. I will knock on the door when I am done."

Kian handed Annani her robe and leaned over Syssi, kissing her lightly on her parched lips. "I love you," he whispered before leaving the room and closing the door behind him.

Out in the hallway, Kian was greeted by eight worried, questioning faces. All of the guardians and Michael were still there. The trays of half-eaten food and the blankets strewn out on the floor were a testament to their resolve to stay.

"There's still no change," Kian told them as he leaned his back against the closed door and crossed his arms over his chest, waiting until a discreet knock from inside the room signaled it was okay for him to come back.

"It is done. Syssi should start getting better now. Take a seat, Kian. It might take a while."

As he plopped tiredly onto the chair and stretched his long legs in front of him, Kian wanted to feel elated at Syssi's increased prospects of making it through the transition, but thoughts of Amanda were keeping him grim.

"I know you are worried about your sister, but I have reason to believe she is not in danger," Annani said softly as she brushed her knuckles over Syssi's flushed cheek.

"What makes you say that?" Kian straightened in his chair.

"I dozed off on the plane and dreamt of her. Amanda was lying in an old-fashioned bathtub and smiling. She did not look worried or afraid." Annani turned back to Syssi and placed her palm over Syssi's forehead. "I think she is cooling down."

"How can you be certain of this? It was only a dream."

"I know the difference between a regular dream and a remote viewing, Kian. You should know better than to doubt me."

"I'm sorry, you're right. I shouldn't. You've certainly proven some of your dreams are more than just dreams. It's just hard for me to rely on visions... But even if Amanda is fine at the moment, and I'm tremendously relieved that she is, there is no guarantee she will remain this way. We still need to find her as soon as we can."

"We will."

42

MICHAEL

"Kri." Michael kissed the sleeping girl's warm cheek.

"Yeah? I'll get right on it…" she mumbled with her eyes still closed.

"Wake up, sweetheart, you're dreaming."

She lifted an eyelid. "What?"

"I just wanted to tell you I'm going to look for some Motrin. I'll be right back. I didn't want you to wake up and wonder where I am."

"Why, what's wrong?" She sat up.

"I've got a headache, and my gums are bothering me." He had been trying to brave it out for the last couple of hours, but the pain was becoming unbearable.

"Ask Bridget, she might have some… and if not, the guys in the lobby will surely have it…" Kri waved him off and plopped back down onto the blanket, letting her eyelids slide shut.

Bridget had her hands full with Syssi, and the last thing Michael wanted was to bother her with his inconsequential toothache.

Taking the elevator up to the lobby, he stood in front of the mirrored wall and tried to see what was going on in his mouth. Stretching his jaw as far as he could, he checked his teeth. But he saw nothing besides some swelling that he wasn't even sure was actually there.

I need a dentist.

But as far as he knew, other than Bridget, there were no other doctors at the keep. And he was pretty sure that leaving to see a human dentist was out of the question.

Shit, I hope they have Motrin.

The guy at the front desk gave him a pitying look and pulled out a packet of pills from his drawer. "Here you go." He handed Michael the square plastic packet, then added a bottle of water. "Hope it helps, kid."

"Thanks, man. Appreciated."

On his way back down, Michael emptied the whole packet of Motrin into his mouth and washed it down with the bottle of water.

When he got to the clinic's level, he didn't go back to sit next to Kri. Instead, he paced the winding corridor, waiting for the pills to kick in.

43

KIAN

When Kian shifted once again in an effort to find a more comfortable position on the rigid chair, Annani frowned. "You should ask someone to roll a gurney in here and catch a few hours of sleep. I will wake you if there is any change."

"It'll be of no use. I'm too worried to fall asleep, but there is no reason for you to suffer as well. I'm sure you'd appreciate a comfortable bed after your long plane ride. Though, don't take it the wrong way; I'm not kicking you out. You're welcome to stay."

"I will stay and keep you company for a little longer. I am not tired at all. The nap I took on the plane was very restful. Did you know it was my first time using the new jet? And I must say, it is a wonderful little thing. The two main seats recline and turn into beds. Can you imagine that on such a small airplane? It even has a shower in addition to the standard facilities. Now that I know I can fly in such comfort, I might visit Sari, Amanda and you more often." Annani glanced at him, checking to see if he liked the idea.

Funny, how she'd done it in a roundabout way, as if not sure of her welcome.

"I wondered when you'd begin to venture away from your sanctuary and travel a little farther than the nearest populated town. I, for one, am always happy to see you, as are the rest of our people. You literally brighten our world…"

"You know I love it there. Why would I want to leave my own paradise? And anyway, I cannot bear to be away from my little ones for long. They are the joy of my life, and I will miss them too much. It has been so long without any children at my place, and now I have two new sweet babies and a toddler boy. You should come visit me and spend some time surrounded by their adorable sounds and smells. It would do you a world of good."

"I wish I could, but my workload is becoming impossible. I have so much to do, I feel guilty every time I steal a few hours to be with Syssi. It's ridiculous." Kian pushed out from the chair and started pacing again, his fingers raking his messed up hair.

"My darling, sweet boy, that is because you are still doing things the way you were doing them two hundred years ago. It was okay to do everything by yourself when things were simpler, and we were not as diversified. But thanks mainly to you, we've become huge. You have to hire professional help, have a team of directors to manage each arm of our holdings separately and report to you. It would free a large chunk of your time to do as you please. You may even decide to study business management at a university." She looked at him hopefully.

It was a conversation they had before; his mother suggesting he should get some form of formal education and him maintaining that he didn't need it and didn't have time for it.

Kian had never gotten to study in any learning institution, higher or lower. What he knew, he had learned from Annani and on his own, and in his opinion, it was enough. If he wanted to learn something new, there were books available on nearly every topic, and the few times he'd needed further explanations, he'd found a leading authority in the field to teach him.

Less time-consuming and way more efficient.

The main advantage of going to any kind of school was socializing, which was fine for the young with no responsibilities on their shoulders. But that didn't mean that graduating from some college or university made them experts or necessarily qualified them for the job.

Only experience did that.

"I don't know if I can trust others enough to relinquish control to them.

And anyway, I don't know where to find qualified people. That undertaking alone will take time I don't have." He paused his pacing to look at her stubborn expression and knew she wouldn't let it go.

"We have several young clan members who have graduated with honors from top universities. Two with Masters in business management, one with a degree in industrial management, and one with a law diploma specializing in business. And those are just the top ones. There are others who may be not as studious but are just as qualified. I can send them your way for interviews."

"How do you know all that?"

"I keep tabs on my progeny. They all spent their early childhoods in my sanctuary, and I care about them and what they do with themselves after they leave." She smiled. "Being called the mother of the clan means more to me than just an honorific or a figure of speech," Annani added with pride.

"In that case, sure... Maybe the time has come to let the younger generation show what they can do..." Kian plopped down on the chair, letting his head drop on his fists.

Annani went on, "Another advantage of hiring the young professionals will be quelling the simmering disquiet in the ranks. Many are frustrated, thinking that our top management positions would always be unattainable to them. You need to demonstrate that you are willing to share the spotlight with others and let more of the clan members climb up and have important jobs."

Annani seemed to have the thirty-thousand-foot view he lacked, and evidently, was much better informed. He should have known what was going on under his nose; should have been more connected to his people. But be that as it may, right now he was too depleted to get energized by the prospect of doing things differently, or to plan a shift in his management style.

"I gave you a lot to think about, so you would not be bored when I leave. Let me know if anything changes. I will be up at Amanda's penthouse." Annani slid down from the hospital bed. "No, do not get up; it is easier for me to kiss you when you are sitting." She took his face in her small, delicate hands and kissed him on both cheeks.

Kian covered her hands with his. "I want to keep your presence here a secret from everyone but the Guardians and council members. So make sure to use only the dedicated penthouse elevator, and if you need anything, send Onidu for it. I don't want someone noticing your servants and figuring out you're here. Keep them at Amanda's place. Please." Too used to issuing orders, he checked himself at the end. This kind of tone wouldn't do with his mother. Even under extenuating circumstances.

Annani nodded at him imperiously and headed for the door.

Once she'd left and he was alone again with Syssi, Kian moved the chair closer to the bed, and holding her hand, rested his cheek on her soft palm. Comforted by the touch he closed his eyes, and in no time, the monotone sounds of the monitoring equipment lulled him to sleep.

It couldn't have been more than a few minutes when the sense of someone creeping around the room woke him up. He jumped, alarmed and ready to pounce on the intruder. But as the cobwebs of his dreamless slumber cleared and his mind registered who had made the sounds that woke him up, Kian slumped back into his chair and blew out a relieved breath.

"You scared the crap out of me, jumping like that!" Bridget held her hand over her racing heart. "I thought you were asleep."

The spike in adrenaline used up what little boost he'd gotten from his few minutes of sleep, and Kian felt just as exhausted as he had been before. "I was..." He sighed.

"I brought you your breakfast—courtesy of Okidu. It's on the rolling tray behind you, but be careful when you reach for it; the coffee is hot."

"Thank you."

Pulling the cart to him, Kian lifted the coffee mug to his lips and took a few sips of the hot brew. "How is Syssi doing? Any improvement?"

"Much better. Her fever is almost back to normal, and her blood pressure has stabilized. Heart is doing well; brainwaves are fine... By the look of it, she is dreaming. She should be waking up any time now. Just as soon as her body is done accommodating the main changes that are taking place."

Turning away from Syssi, Bridget looked him over, and with a hand on her hip, cast him a disapproving look. "Kian, you need to eat, drink, wash your face... No offense, but you look like shit. I have toothbrushes in the bathroom cabinet. Use one!" she ordered, pointing a finger at the bathroom door and waiting till he returned from freshening up, then scowled at him until he took several bites of his sandwich.

Satisfied, she opened the door to leave just as William poked in his flushed face. "I've got it!" he exclaimed, and pushing past Bridget shoved a tablet at Kian.

Frowning at the guy, Kian whispered, "Slow down and keep your voice down... What is it?"

"Sorry," William continued in a hushed, breathless tone. "I checked the security camera recordings from all of the stores I could hack... on and around Rodeo Drive... Amanda's last known location... My boys helped... It was really hard to find all of them... and then it took a long time... to go through all that footage... But we got it... Press the play arrow on the tablet... and see for yourself... I just wish there was an audio... but at least we have the face... of her kidnapper." William's relatively short explanation was delivered between one pant and another. Evidently, the guy had exerted himself running all the way from his lab with his exciting news.

With Bridget and William hovering behind his shoulders, Kian braced for what he was about to see.

It began with what he immediately recognized as a Doomer entering the store, up until the hulking guy had left with Amanda. Kian replayed it two more times, starting with Amanda's terrified expression when she had seen the Doomer, through the disturbingly sexual way she had reacted to his bite, and ending with her leaning her head on his shoulder when they had left the store. It wasn't her fault, Kian kept reminding himself, sickened by the overtly sexual display—she had been high on the venom and had no control over her reactions.

"Interesting..." Bridget commented from behind his back before quickly turning away.

"Interesting? That's what you have to say about it?" Already livid from what he had seen, Kian lashed out at her for what he considered to be a grossly inappropriate response.

"I apologize. I know how disturbing it must have been for you to watch this. It's just that it was the first time I had an opportunity to observe the way it works between an immortal male and female, and couldn't help but be fascinated by the physiology of it. I wasn't commenting on the fact that

Amanda was kidnaped, and that we fear for her safety... Of course, I'm distraught over it."

"What the hell was so fascinating?"

"You've experienced women's reaction to the venom, Kian. But I haven't... I... just wondered how it would feel... I'm sorry..." Bridget blushed and turned away.

Her discomfort finally clued him in. The woman had been aroused by what she had seen. Rationally, he could understand her yearning for that which she couldn't have, but emotionally he was repulsed by her response. Afraid his disgust would show on his face, he turned to William.

"Good job, William, give Onegus a good close-up of the fucker's face, and have him distribute the picture to each of the Guardians and the police."

"I will. Is there anything else I can do?"

"If there is, I cannot think of it now. Go get some sleep, you look beat." It was already late morning, and judging by the guy's red eyes, he had spent the whole night staring at computer screens.

44

YAMANU

*P*ropped against the clinic's hallway wall, Yamanu glanced up from the book he had been reading to see Michael winding between the bodies of Guardians sleeping on the carpeted floor.

The kid was heading his way.

"Yamanu, I need your help, man." Michael's pained voice grabbed his mentor's immediate attention.

"What's wrong?"

"I think I need to see a dentist, and I'm not allowed to leave. Is there anybody you could bring in here? I wouldn't ask, but I can't take it anymore. I took Motrin and it did nothing for the pain… I don't know what else to do…" The poor kid looked tortured.

"Let me see… Open your mouth…" Yamanu took a peek. "Don't be a wuss…," he said as Michael flinched away from his finger, then gently probed the guy's swollen gums. "Just as I thought…" Yamanu grinned and clapped Michael's back. "Welcome to immortality… You're growing fangs and venom glands, and it hurts like a son of a bitch. I know, I still remember it as if it happened last week, though it was ages ago. It was that bad."

Michael remained speechless, his mouth still gaping as he stared at Yamanu's happy face in shocked disbelief. "You're shitting me, right?" he finally said.

"No, I'm not. But let's ask the good doctor's opinion if you don't trust mine." Yamanu took Michael by the shoulders and turned him toward Bridget's office.

"Hold on, I want Kri to come with us…" Michael walked over to where she was sleeping on the floor.

"Kri… wake up, sweetheart. I have great news." Michael brushed his hand over her arm.

Kri sat up with a start. "Did they find Amanda? Did Syssi wake up?"

"No, unfortunately not… But Yamanu thinks I'm transitioning, and we are going to see Doctor Bridget to confirm it. I would really like for you to be there with me."

With a sudden surge of energy, she got up and hugged him tightly. "Oh, Michael! This is wonderful. I can't believe it… I'm so happy for you."

"I'm happy for *us*…" The kid grinned.

Puppy love. Yamanu rolled his eyes.

45

KIAN

*N*auseous with fatigue, Kian finished his coffee and took a few more bites of the sandwich, making an effort to shove some food down his tight throat and into his empty stomach. But swallowing was a pain, and he dropped it back on the plate.

With a grimace, he kicked the rolling cart away.

Turning back to Syssi, he enfolded her small hand with his own, and closing his eyes, rested his forehead on her open palm.

For a moment, he wasn't sure whether what he'd felt was real or his imagination playing tricks on him, but he could've sworn he had felt Syssi's finger brush lightly over his cheek.

Slowly, he lifted his head, hopeful, and yet afraid it was just a phantasm.

Her eyes were open, and as a profound sense of relief washed over him, the small, pitiful smile she managed for him was the most beautiful sight he had ever seen.

She lifted her arm with marked effort, reaching for his cheek. "Wha…" She tried to talk but managed only a croak.

"Hold on, baby. I'll get you something to drink…" Kian rushed over to the tray and poured a glass of water from the pitcher. "I need a straw…" Frantically searching through the cabinets, he found what he was looking for in the one above the sink.

"Here you go, sweetheart…" Kian lifted the head of the bed and brought the straw to her lips. "Slowly, I don't know much about this, but I don't think you should drink a lot at once… Where the hell is Bridget when we need her?" He looked for the call button.

"I'm here." Bridget knocked once before barging in.

"The monitors in my office sounded the alert. Welcome back, Syssi." She smiled.

"Back from where?" Syssi whispered around the straw.

"You've been unconscious since yesterday afternoon, and we've been worried. I'll run some tests and take a blood sample to see where we're at."

Syssi drained the glass. "Did I transition?" she asked hopefully.

"That's what the tests are for. We'll know in a moment." Bridget pulled a syringe and a small surgical knife from the supply cabinet, placing them on her tray.

Kian grabbed her wrist. "What's the knife for?"

"I'm going to make a small cut to see how fast it closes. It's a crude but conclusive test. We'll know right away." She looked at him pointedly, waiting for him to release her.

"It's okay, Kian. I want to know. Let her do it." Syssi extended her arm, offering her palm to Bridget. Then she motioned for Kian to refill her glass with the other.

"Make sure it's tiny and doesn't hurt!" He released Bridget's wrist to pour Syssi more water. Holding the glass with the straw to her lips, he grasped her free hand. "Squeeze my hand if you feel pain."

Bridget rolled her eyes and quickly slashed with her knife.

A line of bright red blood formed over the cut, more of it welling as the seconds ticked away with the three of them watching and holding their breath.

"It's not working…," Syssi whispered, a few tears rolling down her cheeks.

"No, look!" Bridget lifted Syssi's hand, bringing it close to her eyes. "It's closing!" She took a small gauze square from her tray and wiped the blood away. The skin underneath it was already knitting back together, and the small scar faded right before their eyes. In less than a minute, there was no sign of the incision.

"Welcome to immortality, Syssi. To completely transition will take up to six months, but the major change has already taken place. Your body heals itself fast, and it will just keep improving." Bridget smiled at Kian and Syssi's relieved faces. "You're the second one I've welcomed today."

"What?" Kian's eyes shot to her.

"I have Michael in the next room, suffering like a trouper through growing venom glands and fangs. I offered to knock him out and spare him the pain, but he refused. Told me he wants to witness his change. I wonder how long he'll hold out on the painkillers when he realizes it may take up to a month for these beauties to grow." She beamed proudly—as if she had just delivered two new lives into the world. And in a way she had.

"I'm so happy…" Syssi sniffled, returning Kian's gentle embrace.

"Can I take her upstairs now?" Kian asked. If he never had to see the cursed sick room again, it would be too soon.

"Let me just take a few blood samples, and then you're free to go, Syssi. But take it easy until you feel stronger. Small liquid meals to start with, and then nothing heavy for the next twenty-four hours. After that, eat as much as you can stuff into your stomach. You'll need the fuel."

Kian brushed his hand over Syssi's hair. "I'm going to step outside for a minute and tell everybody the good news. They all kept vigil for you, sweetheart. None of the Guardians left this corridor unless they absolutely had to…" He smiled at her and kissed her hand. "It looks like they all have fallen under your spell…" He paused. "My mother flew over to be with you as well, and she wants to meet you as soon as you're up…" He stopped when he saw Syssi's terrified expression.

"She is here?" Syssi whispered. "I can't see her now! I must look like a wreck… Oh my God! She already got to see me looking like this, didn't she?"

"You're being silly. She said you're lovely…"

"I don't care. I want to shower and get dressed before I meet her. Please, Kian, don't let her see me before I do…" Syssi pleaded.

"I won't. I promised to let her know as soon as you were awake, but I'll tell her you want to freshen up… Deal?"

"Thank you!"

. . .

Later, after Bridget was done with her tests and released Syssi into his care, Kian carried her all the way up to his penthouse, despite her protests that she was okay to walk on her own.

Then when he let her down in the bathroom, she shooed him away like some annoying pest. For some inexplicable reason, the mulish woman refused his offer to wash her, insisting she was well enough to do it by herself.

As if that had anything to do with it.

He wanted to take care of her... needed to...

Eventually, he dropped the argument only because he didn't want to upset her so soon after all she had been through.

Waiting, Kian sprawled on his bed, stretching his stiff body as he listened to the sounds percolating from under the bathroom's door; ready to jump to her rescue in case she needed him after all.

But his worry for Amanda pressed heavily on his chest, preventing him from getting any measure of rest, and as his cell phone vibrated in his pocket, he quickly fumbled to pull the thing out; hoping for some good news. "What do you have for me?"

"Kian, we have a situation down at the lobby," Onegus told him. "Martin, the dayshift's security supervisor, called. There is a guy down there, Andrew Spivak, claiming to be Syssi's brother. He demands to see his sister or either Amanda or you. He is making a scene and threatening to bring a SWAT team to storm the building if refused. What do you want me to do?"

"I'm on my way. Tell Martin I'll be there in a few minutes." Kian dropped his legs down the side of the bed and hung his head for a moment. He was so depleted that he couldn't even bring himself to be angry with Syssi for disclosing their location to her brother.

Just another situation for him to handle, he sighed. What else could go wrong? Pushing off the bed, he trudged to the bathroom and opened the door. At the sight of Syssi's delicate body wrapped in a big blue towel, and her long wet hair dripping on the floor, his frustration flew out the window. She looked even smaller and more fragile than before.

With a muted curse, he took her in his arms, and a sense of profound gratitude washed over him as he realized that despite how frail she looked, she was here, alive, and practically indestructible.

Oddly, though, as he held Syssi he felt as if her small, soft body was infusing him with renewed energy, and instead of him lending her his strength, she was his power source.

He kissed the top of her wet hair, filling his lungs with her unique fragrance. "I don't want to rush you, but I just got a call that your brother is down in the lobby and is demanding to see you. I'm going down to talk to him," he said softly.

Syssi seemed just as surprised as he'd been. "How did he find me? Had he had me followed? He must've... after I left the restaurant. I'm so sorry..."

"Well, somehow he has found you. The question is, why is he here? What does he want?"

"He is probably worried about me. I began feeling sick at the restaurant, and he must have called to ask how I felt, then had a conniption when I didn't answer his calls. He is very protective..." Syssi chewed her lower lip, looking troubled. Though Kian wasn't sure what disturbed her more; being the cause for the breach in security or the source of Andrew's angst.

"Don't worry about it, sweetheart. I'll deal with him. Everything is going to be all right." Kian wasn't sure how exactly he would accomplish that, but while she was recovering from her ordeal, he didn't want her upset over anything.

"Maybe I should go down and reassure Andrew that I'm fine. He won't rest until you let him see me anyway. Don't underestimate him, Andrew has his resources. He is an undercover government antiterrorism agent, and before that he was Special Forces."

"In that case, I'd better not have him wait any longer..." Kian smiled at her. "Get dressed. If he wouldn't be satisfied with talking with you on the phone, I'll bring him up here."

"Thank you, I know he'll want to see me."

46

ANDREW

*D*own at the lobby, Andrew paced restlessly, shooting murderous glares at the security people watching his every move. He was beside himself with worry after calling Syssi nonstop for the past two days and leaving urgent messages on her voice mail—to no avail. How sick could she be not to answer any of them, or check her messages? Did this new boyfriend of hers do something to her?

And where was Amanda? He was so sure the woman would take care of Syssi. Why didn't she pick up Syssi's phone?

Andrew's hand went to his concealed weapon.

Don't be an idiot. He dropped his hand back to his side and went back to glaring at the bank of elevators, waiting for the boyfriend to show up, so he could tear him a new ass.

As he waited, several loads of people got out of the elevators. It didn't escape his notice, however, that only two out of the three served the general public. And as soon as the doors of the third one opened, revealing an extraordinarily good-looking man, Andrew knew it was his guy.

It wasn't that Kian and Amanda looked alike, they didn't; Amanda being a brunette and this guy being a reddish, dark blond. But it was the towering height and the level of physical perfection they shared that made it obvious the two were related.

His good looks aside, the man appeared tired, and his haggard appearance made Andrew's gut clench with worry. Dispensing with polite introductions, he pounced on the guy. "Where is my sister? Is she all right?"

"Syssi is fine. She was unwell, but it's all over now, and she's getting better. I'm Kian." The man offered his hand.

"I know." Reluctantly, Andrew shook what he offered. "Andrew Spivak, as I'm sure you were informed by your goons. But although I'm happy to hear Syssi is feeling better, I need to see her with my own eyes..."

47

KIAN

As Kian assessed Andrew, taking in the steely determination and the barely contained aggression wafting off him, he realized Syssi had been right. Her brother would never back off or be placated with a mere phone call. And what's more, Andrew Spivak didn't seem like the type to issue empty threats he had no way of backing up either. Kian had no doubt that if denied an audience with his sister, the guy would come back with a SWAT team and storm the building.

"I sympathize. I have three sisters of my own... Come, I'll take you to see her." Kian led the way toward the elevators.

He couldn't believe he was allowing a practical stranger into his sanctum sanctorum.

Well, whatever. He could always thrall the man to forget the place later. And besides, this was Syssi's brother, which made him part of the family... Sort of.

And yet, even though these were all valid excuses for his easy acquiescence to Andrew's demands, Kian suspected the real reason behind his caving in so quickly was his fatigue. He was just too tired to argue.

As soon as the doors closed, Andrew pinned Kian with a hard stare. "Sorry about the goon remark, I know your people were just doing their job.

But why the high level of security? What kind of business are you running that demands it?" he asked, his eyes holding Kian's with relentless scrutiny.

Kian countered, leveling Andrew's unflinching stare with a hard one of his own. "I assure you there is nothing nefarious about our conglomerate, besides enemies who wish to destroy it and my family along with it." Kian crossed his arms over his chest, his hard frown daring Andrew to further his insulting insinuations.

"Okay then." Andrew nodded his acceptance of Kian's brief explanation, then mirroring Kian's pose, leaned against the elevator's wall and crossed his arms over his chest and his legs at the ankles.

"That's it? No more questions? I would've expected more from someone like you." Kian exited into the penthouse's vestibule, holding the elevator's door open for Andrew.

"For now, it will do… I know when people lie to my face, and you were telling the truth…"

Kian opened the door to his home and motioned Andrew to go ahead. "That's a very useful talent to have."

"I know." Andrew looked around the place with appreciative eyes. "Nice place you got."

"Thank you." Kian closed the door behind them. "Please, make yourself at home while I get Syssi." He pointed to the couch.

Andrew was about to sit down when he got caught with his butt in midair as Syssi rushed in at full speed to hug him fiercely. "I'm so sorry I had you worried. They held me for observation down at the clinic, and my phone was up here. Kian was with me the whole time I was sick, so no one heard it ringing. We just came back up here a short time before you showed up and didn't have the chance to check yet…"

"That's okay; I just need to know how you're doing now."

"I'm all better. It was just a nasty twenty-four-hour bug."

48

ANDREW

Syssi had lied.

Though looking her over, Andrew had no idea why, and about what. He was there when she had gotten sick, and it was obvious that she was recovering from something. But aside from looking tired and thinner, Syssi seemed fine. There were no visible bruises or other signs of injury he could detect.

"By the way, Andrew, how did you find us? Syssi tells me that she didn't share with you where she was staying..." Kian sat down on the couch and stretched his arms on its back.

Shit. I'm screwed.

Rushing over, worried and angry, he hadn't thought of coming up with a plausible story.

Fuck! Syssi was going to blow up. Except, there was not much he could do about it now. He was cornered into admitting the truth.

"I checked your location, Syssi, right after you called me with that story of working from Amanda's place. There is a tracking device in the necklace I gave you for your sweet sixteen. The one you swore you'd always wear." Andrew frowned. "The one I don't see around your neck. Where is it?"

Syssi gaped at him, then as the implication of what he had told her sank in, she narrowed her eyes and flushed red.

175

Andrew winced. Syssi looked so furious that he wouldn't have been surprised if she grabbed something and threw it at him.

"You always do stuff like this. I'm really sick of it. When are you going to start treating me like an adult?" Syssi pushed up from the couch and turned her back to him.

Andrew suppressed a smile. Ever since she'd been a toddler, Syssi would always do that; refuse to look at him when he made her mad. "I don't know why you're so angry with me... It's just a location tracker. And it's not like I'm spying on what you're doing or listening in on your conversations. In my opinion, everybody should have one. Even I have a tracker on me at all times... It's a perfectly reasonable precaution." Andrew pushed up from where he was sitting and placed his hands on Syssi's shoulders.

She shrugged them off.

"Some help here?" He shot Kian a pleading look, hoping the boyfriend might hold more sway.

"Andrew is absolutely right. I wish I had Amanda wear a tracking device. I wouldn't be sitting here helpless if I had." Kian grimaced.

Syssi turned to Kian, her face suddenly lined with worry. "Why? What happened to Amanda?"

"Yes, where is Amanda? What's going on?" Andrew echoed, his gut clenching.

Kian's pained expression confirmed his fear. "After she left the restaurant where you three had lunch yesterday, she was abducted. We found a recording from a surveillance camera at the jewelry store she was taken from, so we know it was one of our enemies who took her. But that's all we have. We don't even know where to begin looking." Kian sank into the couch cushions, hanging his head on his fists.

The distressing news sliced through Andrew like a serrated blade, tearing up his gut. He knew all too well what could befall such a beautiful woman in captivity—the images, unfortunately, made vivid by the many others he had witnessed during his time on the force.

"Oh my God. Oh my God..." Syssi repeated frantically, her hand flying to her throat.

"Oh! My! God!" she exclaimed more forcefully as her eyes popped wide open.

Bewildered, Andrew glanced at Kian, whose questioning expression echoed his own.

"Amanda has my necklace, Andrew! My sweet, overprotective brother! You're my hero! She was wearing my necklace! You can find her!" Syssi jumped on him, hugging him with all she had.

It took a few seconds for her words to sink in, and as they did, Andrew felt Kian's hands on his shoulders, turning him around and pulling him into a brief embrace.

"I'll be forever in your debt for this. Thank you!" Kian sounded hoarse.

Overwhelmed by Kian's infectious hope, Andrew took a step back. "I haven't found her yet…" A hope he was loath to disappoint. Unfortunately, experience had taught him that not every rescue mission ended with success.

"I'll assemble a team with some of my buddies from my old unit. That was what we did, hostage retrieval. I will get her back for you," Andrew offered, praying he would be able to deliver on that promise: more for Amanda's sake than Kian's. But it had to be handled with extreme care. In a situation like this, even a seemingly insignificant mistake could have fatal consequences.

Kian placed a hand on Andrew's shoulder. "I truly appreciate the offer, but all I need from you is her location. My men and I will handle the rest. We have reason to believe her kidnapper is acting on his own behalf, and no one else is involved. It's not like we have to invade another country or storm a stronghold and need a trained commando unit to do the job. He is just one man."

Andrew's anger bubbled up like hot tar. Was the idiot concerned with honor or appearances when his sister's life was on the line?

"You listen closely now, as I'm going to say it only once." Andrew got in Kian's face. "I'm heading the rescue with my people, and you can tag along… if you can follow orders. This is not a job for amateurs, regardless of any combat training you might have, or how much you care about Amanda, or how easy you believe it would be. My men and I are trained and experienced in exactly these kinds of situations. If anybody has a chance to bring her back in one piece, it is me. Don't you dare indulge in playing power games when the stakes are this high. Do we have an understanding?"

49

KIAN

Kian gritted his teeth, knowing Andrew was right and resenting him for it. It was irrational, even stupid, to feel this way about the man with the means and know-how that were crucial for Amanda's rescue. But he loathed the necessity to relinquish control over the situation to an outsider.

"Fine! You lead, and you can bring two of yours. But I'm coming with two of mine... You need us; there are things only we know about our enemies," Kian growled, and pulled out his phone. "Tell me what you need and I'll arrange for it."

"I'll call my friend, have him swing by my place and bring my laptop. Once we know more about where the perp is holding her, we can form a plan of action. We'll need a private room for our people to meet and plan the mission."

"Have your guy come to the lobby. I'll have a room ready by the time he gets here."

"Good."

As Andrew stepped out to the terrace to make his calls, Syssi tagged behind him. "I need a cigarette..." She grabbed the pack that was still out on the side table next to the chaise.

Andrew arched a brow but said nothing. Turning his back to her, he kept talking with his man in a hushed voice.

Joining Syssi on the lounger, Kian wrapped his arm around her shoulders. "It must've been difficult to grow up with a badass like him." He smirked. "Compared to Andrew's raging bull style, I'm merely a housebroken bulldog. Not that I'm not grateful beyond words for his help…"

"I know, right? Now you know why your he-man antics have no effect on me. I have lots of experience dealing with that." Syssi playfully bumped his shoulder with her head.

"Imp…" Kian cupped her neck, and holding her pressed against him, buried his nose in her hair.

Syssi sighed. "Andrew had to take charge. With our parents always busy elsewhere, he practically raised my younger brother and me. But he is a great guy, and I love him. I bet once you're done with your macho posturing, you guys will get along great… He cares about Amanda, you know… Yesterday at that lunch there was definitely something going on between them."

"You know Amanda. She would flirt with a wooden post… It doesn't mean anything." Kian sighed, missing his sister with all her little annoying habits and her never-ending drama. He would never admit it, but he enjoyed all that brouhaha she created around her. She was fresh, and fun, and lively… Oh hell, he really hoped his mother's vision was true…

"Perhaps…" Syssi said. "I had a feeling it was more than that, though. It looked like they really liked each other. Found each other interesting, beyond the physical attraction. It wasn't just Amanda's usual act." Syssi took a drag on her cigarette, collecting her thoughts. "I want to tell Andrew the truth. He has to have all the facts if he is to bring Amanda home safely. Besides, as my brother, he is also a Dormant. You should offer him the same deal you offered Michael and me."

Kian ran his fingers through his hair and grimaced. "You're right. He should know. Although I hate to do it under these circumstances. What if he refuses the offer? I can't thrall him until after the mission without compromising him, and in the meantime, he'll have us by the balls."

"You can trust Andrew. He'd never do anything to endanger my safety, and I'm one of you now."

"I can just imagine his response…" Kian chuckled. "Who is going to lay it on him?"

"I'll do it. But you'll have to supply the details and the proof. Regrettably, I don't have fangs to show him or the ability to create illusions. Or do I?" Syssi looked at him hopefully.

"I don't know. You might. I'll try to explain how it is done once things get back to normal." Kian leaned into her, taking her mouth in a hungry kiss. "I can't wait for us to enjoy ourselves with each other without some calamity hanging over our heads…" he whispered once he let go of her lips.

"Me either," Syssi whispered throatily.

"I can't believe you two are making out at a time like this!" Andrew snapped. "Can't you control yourselves?"

Syssi and Kian exchanged knowing glances.

"Take a seat, Andrew. There is something I need to tell you, and you'd better be sitting for this." Syssi gestured toward the lounger across from them.

"Don't tell me you're pregnant and running off to Vegas to get married…" Andrew looked them over, his expression only half-joking.

"No, I'm not pregnant. Not yet, anyway…" Syssi smiled at Kian and winked, teasing Andrew for sounding like an old prude. "But I did go through an interesting change recently… a change you might consider for yourself."

"What are you talking about?" Andrew frowned. "Let me guess… A fanatic cult? Self-help nonsense? New health diet?" He taunted his sister with his absurd suggestions.

"No, and stop it. You're not playing nice. But anyway, back to what I was trying to say. I wish I could tell you all of this under less stressful circumstances, but we decided that it is important for you to know what you're dealing with on this mission. So here it goes…" Syssi took a long breath, bracing for what she was about to reveal.

"Kian, Amanda, and the rest of their extended family, as well as their enemies, including the one that abducted Amanda, are the descendants of the gods of old. They are near immortal, immune to all mortal diseases, and can regenerate from all but the most severe injuries, which makes them almost indestructible. Also, some of them have the ability to cast very convincing illusions; fooling mortal minds into believing whatever they project. Their own minds are resistant to that kind of manipulation, so they cannot fool each other... Do you understand now why a team of mortals would fail against this kind of an opponent? That's why you need Kian and his men with you."

Andrew stared at Syssi as if she had lost her mind, then turned to Kian with what looked like an intent to harm. "What kind of drugs have you been feeding her?"

"Would you like a demonstration? Hand me the knife you have strapped to your calf, and I'll prove it to you."

"Are you nuts? I'm not going to give you my knife..."

"If I wanted to do you harm, it would have been already done. I need the knife to cut myself. I think what you'll see will convince you."

Still shaking his head, Andrew pulled the knife from the holster strapped to his calf and handed it to Kian. "Knock yourself out..."

Kian ran the sharp blade over the inside of his forearm, watching the blood well. The cut closed itself almost as soon as he made it, the small scar disappearing a few seconds later.

"Wow, you healed much faster than I did. Is it because your blood is purer?" Syssi looked amazed at the speed with which his body had regenerated.

Kian nodded, affirming her assumption. "Do you need more proof?" He turned to Andrew. "I can project Godzilla, or Spider-man, or anyone else you could think of... Take your pick."

"If it weren't my own knife, I would have thought it was a trick... I've never seen anything like that... But just for kicks... humor me with an illusion." Andrew shook his head. "What you claim is so out there, I feel I need more to be convinced it's for real."

"Anything in particular?" Kian smirked.

"Surprise me..."

"Okay, here is one I haven't done in a while..."

Andrew's eyes almost popped out of their sockets at the sight of the huge Phoenix bird that appeared in Kian's place. Syssi, on the other hand, was still looking at where it perched on the chaise as if she was waiting for something to happen.

181

"You can't see it anymore, sweetheart. Your mind is now immune to thralls and illusions. But if you close your eyes and focus, you'll see it." Kian smirked at Andrew's shocked expression when the guy heard him talk out of the bird's beak.

"Okay, you can drop the bird. I believe you... Explain why Syssi couldn't see it?"

So the guy wasn't completely stupefied and noticed their telltale exchange.

"That's because she was turned into one of us. She, and you as her brother, are rare possessors of our dormant genes, which we can activate. You are only the second Dormant male we've discovered, with Syssi being the first and only female, and as the rest of us are all related, that makes you a very valuable asset, especially to the females of our clan. Until now, their only choice of partners were mortals, with all the limitation that entailed. I'll spare you the history and the complicated explanation. When we get Amanda back, she'll fill in the details. It's her field of expertise."

"So what are you saying? Syssi is immortal now, and you intend to turn me as well?" Andrew frowned.

"No one will force you to do it. It's your choice. But why would you choose not to? Are you so tired of living that you would refuse near-immortality?" Kian arched his brow.

As he regarded Kian, Andrew's expression revealed his skepticism. "I need to know more. I'm sure there is a catch somewhere. Like selling my soul to the devil or something like that. There is never something offered for nothing."

"You'll get all the info after the mission and will have time to decide. The transition is not easy on the body, and it seems that the older the body, the harder it gets. So you cannot attempt it now. You have a team to lead. But after..." Still holding the blade, Kian raised his hands in the air to indicate the open possibility.

Andrew took it back and returned it to its holster, then pushed up from the lounger. "We have a rescue to plan... Or do you lovebirds need some more time alone?" He grimaced at the sight of their entwined hands.

"We do, but time is not on our side..." Kian kissed Syssi's hand and leaned to whisper in her ear. "Tell Okidu when you're ready to see my mother. You don't want to offend her by making her wait too long. And by the way, only the Guardians and council members know she is here, and, of course, the Odus. I want to keep it this way. So don't mention it to anyone besides them." He kissed her cheek before pushing off to stand.

"I'll be back to fill you in on the details after we formulate the plan." Kian cast one last glance at Syssi's concerned face before heading out with Andrew.

Once Kian had closed the door behind them, Andrew pinned him with hard eyes. "If I can trust my judgment about you at all, after that little demonstration of yours, I think you love my sister. And in that case, you have my blessing. But if you ever hurt her..."

"Yeah, yeah... You'll chop me into small pieces. I get it... No worries, Andrew. I'm going to spend my very long life loving Syssi and protecting her from all harm. You have my word."

50

SYSSI

*N*othing could have prepared Syssi for Annani's splendor. The goddess's radiance and palpable power were so overwhelming that she had an urge to curtsy.

Instead, she bowed her head respectfully.

"Oh, my dear girl, you look so much better already. Poor Kian was going out of his mind with worry. He loves you very much… Come, sit with me." Annani took Syssi's hand, leading her to sit on Amanda's couch much in the same way her daughter had done.

"So, how do you feel? Anything different?" She patted Syssi's hand in a motherly gesture that belied her much-too-young appearance.

It was really disconcerting, this dichotomy between the goddess's youthful looks and the ancient power and wisdom of her eyes. But surprisingly, there was also mischief and liveliness in them—more so than in the eyes of her much younger progeny.

"There is nothing truly significant. I feel healthy and vital, and my senses are sharper than they used to be. I hear and see better and smell… that's actually the weirdest part; I think I can smell emotions. Am I imagining it?"

"No, my dear, you are not imagining the smells. The body secretes different hormones for different emotions and each has its own unique smell, some more pungent than others…" Annani chuckled and winked at her.

Syssi peered down at their entwined hands. *What do I say next? How do you conduct a conversation with a goddess?*

Annani was friendly and her smile was genuine. But it was impossible to forget what she was. She was freaking aglow! And not in the metaphorical sense!

"Come on, Syssi, you must have thousands of questions. Ask away. You are going to become the mother of a new clan—our best hope for the future of the last five thousand years. I am here to guide you and help you, so you do not have to do it all on your own. My vast experience is at your disposal." Annani gave Syssi's hand a reassuring squeeze.

"Oh, my God, when you put it like that, it terrifies me. I'm not ready to become this queen bee. I pray Amanda finds more female Dormants, so I can share this burden with others. I don't think I can handle that much responsibility on my own." Syssi kept her eyes downcast, ashamed of her cowardice.

"I hope there will be more like you too, but it is beside the point. When I started on this journey, I was an immature, spoiled girl with no idea of what would be required of me. I stepped up to the plate, and so will you, but with the added benefit of my guidance and help. I am older than most civilizations, you know. There is very little I have not seen or done…" She joggled both brows suggestively.

Syssi had to smile, Annani reminded her so much of Amanda with her outrageous persona. "How do you do that? After all this time and all you have seen, you still have your sense of humor and a glint of excitement in your eyes. I get depressed reading the headline news… There is so much suffering and misfortune out there… I find it hard to stomach. It weighs me down."

"The answer to that is multifaceted." Annani's demeanor turned serious. "You read the news and feel powerless to do anything to make it better. You can only bear witness to all that suffering, and that helplessness depresses you. I, on the other hand, am fortunate to have the means to change this world for the better. And although we suffered many setbacks through the millennia, and the progress is slow, things are getting better. As my efforts bear fruit, I feel fulfilled. I have hope. My dream lives. That is the major source of my happiness, the knowledge that good will prevail in no small part because of me..."

Annani paused, and a bright smile enlivened her perfect face as she continued. "And there are my little ones, my great-grandchildren. I am surrounded daily by their innocence and their unconditional love. I see them grow and blossom into wonderful people... well, most of them anyway... They fill my heart with love and pride. And last but not least, I make sure to have fun... if you know what I mean... lots of fun..." Annani's voice dropped an octave, her demeanor reverting to playful and mischievous.

Then she smiled like an old sage and squeezed Syssi's hand. "So you see, my darling, what I was trying to do with my long-winded speech about my fabulous self—was guide you to your new destiny. You are not helpless anymore; you are no longer a powerless witness to evil; now, you are part of the force for good. But as wonderful as having a purpose and working toward your goals is, the heart needs more to thrive. You have a wonderful man to love, to look after and to guide. I know you think you are too young and inexperienced and wonder what guidance you could possibly provide someone like Kian. But he needs you more than either of you realize. My darling son feels like poor Atlas, carrying the weight of the world on his shoulders, and he needs you to lend him yours."

"I'll do what I can... I have a minor in business and could possibly take over some of his less important tasks. Though I don't think I'll be much help really. I have a lot to learn before I'd be of any use."

Annani dismissed Syssi's concerns with a wave of her hand. "Oh, I am not talking only about his work. I have already talked him into hiring some of our young professionals for that. But you, my dear, could help him choose the right people for the job. What Kian needs assistance with the most is creating a cohesive team. My son is a natural tactical leader and does great as a commander-in-chief, which served him well in the past when an autocratic style of leadership was the norm. Except, he has never developed the skills necessary for diplomacy and building a strong business team. You, on the other hand, with your sweet nature and humble disposition, could be the glue that binds them together. Everyone likes you; you are approachable."

"Except, I'm not assertive, and I shy away from confrontations. Not exactly the traits of a leader..." Syssi tried and failed to pull her hand out of Annani's grasp.

"Bah, but that is exactly my point. You will balance Kian's excess of those traits. As a cool, logical seer, you will probably hold more sway than my hotheaded, obnoxious son."

Syssi regarded her with wary eyes. "I'm not exactly a seer, and Kian is not that obnoxious..."

"So, I have exaggerated a little... Your precognition ability is a very rare gift, even among my kind. And in all likelihood, it will grow progressively stronger now that you have transitioned. And as to my son... Kian takes after me. Being obnoxious runs in the family." Annani laughed, the musical chimes sound of her laughter so beautiful it raised goose bumps on Syssi's arms.

She chuckled. "If you say so..."

"Yes, I know what they say about me: the good and the bad. Anyway, back to what I was trying to explain. You have to have balance in your life and not forget to have fun. Those who neglect that crucial ingredient in the long run become more dead than alive. So make sure to make fun a priority for you and my son." Annani winked and squeezed the hand she wouldn't let go of.

"I hope Kian and I will be happy with each other. Though I don't know how we are going to keep our love and passion fresh. With so many years ahead of us, is it even possible?"

"This is the beauty of our peculiar physiology. You will crave each other above all others and always find bliss in each other's arms. But that is only the physical part, the rest is up to you. Tragically, I lost my love at the start of our lives together, so I do not have personal experience with long-term relationships. But I was fortunate enough to witness some wonderfully fulfilling truelove matings, and even some of the arranged marriages blossomed into love and thrived. So to answer your question; yes, it is definitely possible."

"I hope you're right. I love Kian passionately, but we have only just met, and it scares me to think things might change—that I'd make mistakes and ruin it somehow..."

"Do not fret. If the foundation is strong, it will withstand some rattling. It may even provide some spice... after all, making up after a fight is fun..." Annani smiled a knowing little smile.

"Again, I hope you're right..." Syssi sighed.

"Come here, sweet child..." Annani pulled on Syssi's hand with surprising strength for someone so small and seemingly fragile, embracing her tightly. "If my son ever does anything to upset you, he will have me to deal with." She kissed Syssi on both cheeks then leaned back a little and looked into her moist eyes. "As of now, you are my daughter, and I want you to think of me as your second mother. I will always be there for you, even if it means boxing Kian's ears or kicking his posterior occasionally... You hear?"

"Thank you..." Choked up with gratitude at the wholehearted acceptance, Syssi sniffled as tears slid from under her lashes. Never, not in a million years, would she have expected that kind of pledge from the goddess.

From Kian's mother.

51

SYSSI

"*D*id you complain to my mother about me?" Kian asked as he stepped out onto the terrace.

"No, of course not... Why?" Puzzled, Syssi looked up at him.

After leaving Annani, she had gone back to the terrace outside of Kian's penthouse and sat down to smoke another cigarette. Now that health was no longer a concern, she was really letting herself indulge with a promise to quit later once this crisis was over.

Except, she had a strong feeling that it was just the beginning and more trouble was lurking on the horizon. With all the recent turmoil, she had been too preoccupied to let her mind wander aimlessly, and the cursed premonitions had been held at bay. But the moment things returned to normal and resumed a slower pace, she had no doubt her foresight would come rushing back. Perhaps even worse than before, as Annani had predicted.

Oh, the joy.

As obscure as her premonitions tended to be, they were pretty useless, serving only to darken her mood.

"Oh, I don't know... I stopped by Amanda's place to update my mother on the rescue plan we came up with, and she threatened to kick my butt if I ever dared to upset you... Care to explain?" He plopped next to her and kissed her heated cheek.

"Oh, that... It's nothing. Well, not nothing. Your mother has done the sweetest thing; she made me feel so accepted and so welcomed, that I teared up. She pledged to always have my back. Even against you. Can you believe it? I hope that doesn't hurt your feelings..." Syssi gazed up at Kian's tired, smiling face.

"I'm actually elated that she has made such a promise to you. It makes me a happy man to know that my mother cares so much for the woman I love." Kian pulled Syssi close to his body and kissed her with tender, soft lips. "I love you," he whispered into her mouth.

"I love you so much." Syssi sighed. She felt guilty even thinking it—but it was so unfair. Instead of celebrating her successful transition, preferably by making love, Kian was heading for a dangerous rescue mission. The Fates Amanda believed in must've been cruel and capricious, amusing themselves by messing with people's lives.

"Make love to me before you go," she whispered, tugging on Kian's shoulders as she leaned back.

Slipping his arms around her, he held her up and kissed her again. "I can't. Not until I come back."

5 2

KIAN

There was nothing Kian wanted more than to lay Syssi down on that lounger and cover her body with his. Unfortunately, he couldn't allow himself that sweet indulgence. If he made love to Syssi in his exhausted state, he would be worthless for tonight's mission.

"I'm running on fumes."

"And here I thought you were Superman." Syssi chuckled.

"I'm sure even Superman needs a few hours of sleep once in a while."

"Don't look so hurt, I was just joking." She kissed his nose. "You'll always be my Superman."

"I wasn't hurt." *Well, maybe just a little...*

"Aha... sure..." Syssi narrowed her eyes. "Men and their egos. Just promise me you'll be careful and not pull any macho stunts out there. I need you..." Her voice quivered a little. "When are you heading out?"

"We are leaving at midnight," he said, touching his forehead to hers. "The Doomer holds Amanda at a remote mountain cabin, so we cannot risk landing the helicopter anywhere near the place—even with the silent blades. We'll have to trek several miles through the forest for a surprise attack."

"How long do you think it will take?" Syssi whispered in a failed attempt to hide the growing tremor in her voice.

"We estimate it will take us at least two hours to get there on foot. The rest should go down quickly. We'll probably be back before three."

Syssi's worried eyes were getting moist with unshed tears, but she said nothing.

"There are six of us going and only one of him. The Doomer doesn't stand a chance. You have nothing to worry about. Andrew knows what he's doing. His plan, at least on paper, seems fail-proof." Kian did his best to sound more assured than he really was. Even the best of plans sometimes failed. There were always surprises, and unforeseen obstacles could derail the whole thing. It was impossible to account for everything, and the help of the capricious Lady Luck was needed.

"Just bring Amanda home, safely," Syssi whispered. "The lives of the most important people in my life are on the line tonight. I will lose a millennium of my new immortal life until I see all of you safely back," she said with a lone tear sliding down her cheek.

"Oh, baby… Don't cry. I promise we will all come back." He hugged her close.

I'm such a fucking liar, promising what I can't guarantee to deliver.

53

SYSSI

t midnight, Syssi accompanied the men to the rooftop helipad. Outside, dark clouds obscured the moon, casting ominous shadows on the dimly illuminated platform and the large craft perching on top of it. Syssi suppressed a shiver.

It's not a premonition, don't read anything into it!

"Come back home safely, all of you!" She briefly hugged Anandur and Brundar, then crushed Andrew in a desperate hug while choking back tears.

If I lose him too, it will destroy me. I'd rather die than live with that pain again. My new immortality may as well become a curse instead of a blessing.

"Don't worry. We'll be back with Amanda in no time at all." Andrew kissed her forehead, then dislodged himself with effort from her tight embrace. "Damn, you're strong now…" He gave her hands a reassuring squeeze before running under the helicopter's blades to board the craft.

The moment Andrew let go, Kian took her in his arms. "Stay with my mother. You could use each other's support…" he said before kissing the living daylights out of her. "That was just an appetizer. Later tonight, we feast…" Wiping her tears away, he commanded, "Smile!" then shook his head at her pitifully miserable attempt at one. "I think you need another kiss…" He took her lips again.

She held on as he tried to pull away. "Just a little longer..." she whispered.

"Everything is going to be fine, sweet girl," he murmured against her lips as he kissed her again, softly, then with one last squeeze extracted himself from her arms and hurried to the waiting helicopter.

"Good luck!" Syssi called after his retreating back.

Hugging herself against the night's chill, she watched as the helicopter carrying the two men she loved most in the world took off, then banked north. Her vision blurred by tears, she followed the craft's blinking lights until they disappeared in the distance. "Come back safely to me... Please!" She cast her prayer on the cold, indifferent wind.

THE CHILDREN OF THE GODS SAGA CONTINUES WITH AMANDA AND DALHU'S STORMY ENEMIES-TO-LOVERS STORY

Taken by the enemy, Amanda soon discovers that there is more to the handsome Doomer than his dark past and hulking, sexy body.

READ ON FOR A SNEAK PEEK

AMANDA

As she heard Dalhu exhale a relieved breath from behind the bathroom door, Amanda smirked with satisfaction.

Dalhu's surprised expression when he'd burst into the bathroom had been priceless. Seeing her in all her nude glory with her body boldly displayed in the bath's clear water—not gasping or trying to cover herself as most women would—the guy had been rendered speechless.

But then she was nothing like what he was used to.

Not even close.

Amanda was the daughter of a goddess, for fate's sake.

He hadn't been the only one affected, though. As he'd devoured her with his hungry eyes, her body had responded, her nipples growing taut under his hooded gaze.

Ogling her, he'd wiped the drool off his mouth with the back of his dirty hand, looking just as awestruck as one of her students. But that was where the resemblance ended.

Dalhu was a magnificent specimen of manhood, and in comparison, all her former partners looked like mere boys. Shirtless and sweaty, he'd looked just as amazing as she'd imagined he would.

He was big; not even Yamanu was that tall, and Dalhu was more power-fully built. Nevertheless, his well-defined muscles were perfectly proportioned for his size with no excess bulk; he looked strong, but not pumped like someone who spent endless hours lifting weights at a gym.

Following the light smattering of dark hair trailing down the center of his chest to where it disappeared below the belt line of his jeans, she hadn't been surprised to find that he was well proportioned everywhere. And as he kept staring at her, mesmerized, his jeans growing too tight to contain him, she'd held her breath in anticipation of her first glimpse of that magnificent length.

Oh, boy, am I in a shitload of trouble.

There was just no way she could resist all that yummy maleness. Amanda knew she was going to succumb to temptation.

She always had.

Except, this time, she would be stooping lower than ever. Because she could think of nothing that would scream SLUT louder than her going willingly into the arms of her clan's mortal enemy...

Shit, damn, damn, shit... she cursed silently.

It had taken sheer willpower to kick him out. She so hadn't wanted to...

But she would've never been able to look at herself in the mirror if she'd succumbed to the impulse and had dragged him down into that bathtub to have her wicked way with him.

Hopefully, he'd been too busy hiding his own reaction to have noticed hers.

What was it about him that affected her so? Yes, he was incredibly handsome, and she was a lustful hedonist... but, come on, she had been a hair away from jumping the guy...

Was she one of those women that got turned on by bad boys?

Yep, evidently I am.

How shameful...

Her hand sneaked down to the juncture of her thighs, and she let her finger slide over the slick wetness that had nothing to do with the water she was soaking in. But after a quick glance at the door that wouldn't close, she gritted her teeth and pulled her fingers away from the seat of her pleasure.

She couldn't let Dalhu know how he affected her if she hoped to have a chance of keeping him off her.

And herself off him...

Damn!

She had to keep telling herself over and over again, repeating it like a mantra until it sunk in, that there was nothing that would scream SLUT louder than her going willingly into the arms of a Doomer.

Oh fates, I'm such a slut...

But wait... this was it...the solution to her predicament...

If there was one thing that was sure to shatter Dalhu's romantic illusions, it was to find out that the woman he wanted for his mate had been with a shitload of others before him.

She was well acquainted with the Doomers' opinions about women and their place in society. Someone like her would be probably stoned to death in the parts of the world they controlled. And though Dalhu seemed smarter and better informed than the average Doomer, he no doubt believed in the same old double standard. It was perfectly okay for him to fuck a different woman every night because his body demanded it. But it was not okay for her.

She was supposed to suffer the pain like a good little girl because decent women were not supposed to want or enjoy sex...

Well, she not only wanted it and enjoyed it but needed it to survive, just like any other near-immortal male or female.

But try explaining it to a Doomer...

Stupid. Blind. Deaf.

Members of the brotherhood of the "Devout Order Of Mortdh" were brainwashed to hate women and believed them to be inferior and unworthy. It was sad, really, how easy it was for Navuh and his propaganda to affect not only his followers, and not only the male population of the regions under his control, but also the women living there. They succumbed to the same beliefs, accepting that they were inferior, that being abused was their due, and that that was what their God wanted for them.

The poor things didn't know any better.

If a girl heard all throughout her life that she was worthless, and her education was limited to basic literacy at best, she was going to believe it, buying into the label she'd been given and perceiving herself that way.

Thinking back to her own youth in Scotland and even later in their new home in America, the situation for women had been only slightly better.

Though they were not as badly mistreated as their counterparts in Navuh's region, the prevailing attitude, sadly, had been similar up until recent times. Women had been considered not as smart and not as capable as men, but at least their mothering and homemaking skills had been appreciated. For most of her life, women had accepted these beliefs as immutable truths, treating the few that had tried to rise above them as bad mothers, misguided individuals, and an undesirable influence on their daughters.

Thank heavens this was changing. There was still discrimination in the workforce, with men getting better pay and faster promotions, but at least the West was on the right track.

Oh, well, her mother and the rest of their clan did what they could. But where Navuh had his clutches deeply in the hearts of mortals there was nothing to be done.

They were lost souls.

As was Dalhu.

The guy struggled against what he was, though, she had to hand him that. But could he break free after the centuries of brainwashing he'd suffered?

As a scientist, Amanda knew there was no hope for him. But as a person, as a woman... well... hope was for children and fools—as Kian was fond of saying.

She wasn't a child... so that left being a fool...

Still, hopeful or not, how was she going to get the guy disillusioned with her without getting him so enraged that he would chop her head off?

Dalhu was unstable, going from rage to affection in a heartbeat, and she was afraid of what he'd do if she told him the truth about whom he was planning to spend his life with.

Perhaps the smart thing to do was to bide her time and wait to be rescued.

But how would anyone even know where to look for her?

Damn. What to do... what to do...

Wait... but what if she let Dalhu have her...

Just so he wouldn't kill her... of course...

That wouldn't count as her going to him willingly, would it?

And if she didn't suffer horribly in the process... well...

Now that she'd come up with a semi-moral excuse for sleeping with the enemy—only if it became necessary of course—her mood improved, and she hurried to finish soaping, shampooing, and conditioning before Dalhu got tired of waiting and decided to jump in the tub with her.

Having the option didn't mean she should court that particular outcome, did it?

She finished drying off with the cheap, coarse towel and wrapped it around her body with a grimace. It was way too short, barely covering her butt.

Clutching the shitty towel so it would cover at least her nipples on top and the juncture of her thighs on the bottom, she walked out of the bathroom.

"Not a word, Dalhu. Not a fucking word..." she hissed at his ogling smirk, the cuss word feeling foreign and vulgar on her lips.

He arched a brow but said nothing. Grabbing a pair of gray sweats, he tore off the price tags and ducked into the bathroom she'd just vacated.

There was another set of sweats folded on top of the bed... pink... and plain cotton panties... also pink...

Her lips twisted in distaste. "Oh, goody, that must be for me."

With a quick glance behind her, she made sure the bathroom door was closed, or as well as it could be, before dropping the towel. With a sigh, she reluctantly shimmied into the cheap panties and then pulled on the shapeless, polyester-blend sweats.

Her bare skin had never before touched anything as disgusting, and a glance at the mirror hanging over the bathroom door proved that she'd never before worn anything as ugly as this either.

She looked positively... well... blah.

The good news was that no one she knew was going to see her in this humiliating getup. Unfortunately, though, she was pretty sure that it didn't make her look ugly enough for Dalhu to lose interest either.

The bad news was that she had no idea how she was going to sleep with the horrible synthetic fabric irritating her skin. And sleeping naked was not an option—even if she made Dalhu sleep on the couch downstairs.

Sifting through the bags, she found the bedding she'd had him bring from the store. One scratchy sheet went over the naked mattress, then pillowcases over the two pillows, and another sheet under the comforter that, surprise, surprise, was also made from polyester...

Had there been nothing else in that store? Or had Dalhu chosen the worst stuff to torture her with...

Well, payback is a bitch.

Grabbing a pillow and a woven blanket, she hurried down the stairs and dropped them on the couch. The thing was too short for Dalhu's huge body, and hopefully, it was lumpy as well.

"Sleep tight... hope you get lots of bedbug bites..." she singsonged as she walked over to the kitchen.

The food supplies Dalhu had stolen from the store were on the floor, still in their paper bags, and as she began taking the stuff out and arranging it on the counter, her spirits sank even further. Apparently, Dalhu's idea of nutrition was mostly canned meat, canned beans, a few cans of vegetables, sliced white bread, and peanut butter.

The only thing to brighten her mood was a can of ground coffee, but only momentarily—there was no coffeemaker.

Putting together a peanut butter sandwich was something even she could do, but making coffee without the benefit of a coffeemaker was above the level of her meager culinary skills.

A quick search through the cabinets yielded nothing more exciting than some pots and pans, but at least, thank heavens, she found a can opener.

Scooping some of the coffee into a pot, Amanda filled it with water and turned on the electric stove. Trouble was, she had no idea what the ratio should be, or if it was even possible to make stove top coffee.

Hopefully, it would be drinkable...

She was desperate for it.

As she arranged the rest of the supplies in the cabinets, the aroma wafting from the cooking coffee smelled delicious, and once it looked like it was done, she poured it into two cups and began making peanut butter sandwiches for Dalhu and herself.

DALHU

Dalhu glanced at the ridiculously short sweats he'd pulled on after showering. The sleeves reached a little below his elbows, and the shirt's bottom barely covered his bellybutton. He'd pulled and tied the waistband string as tight as it would go, but it was still too wide and the pants kept sliding down. The fucking double X must've been about the girth, not the length.

And it wasn't as if Dalhu was worried about flashing a pair of boxer shorts. He wasn't wearing any. He'd forgotten to include them in his supply procurement…

For a moment, he considered changing into one of the fancy designer jeans that he'd purchased at that Rodeo Drive boutique. The faggot salesman had insisted that they made Dalhu's ass look *fabulous*…

Fortunately, for the bastard, he'd been so helpful and pleasant before the *ass* remark that Dalhu had decided to let him live…

Had it been only this morning?

So much had happened since that he felt as if it had happened days ago.

How much had he paid for those jeans? A thousand? More?

At least he'd paid with a credit card and not cash. On the run, the card was useless and he was low on cash. He kept the card, though, just in case. Hopefully, the Brotherhood's bureaucrats wouldn't cancel it anytime soon.

The designer clothes he'd spent so much money on wouldn't be used for their original purpose, though, and the custom suit he'd ordered would remain unclaimed.

The only reason he'd needed those obscenely expensive clothes in the first place was to go hunting for the males of Amanda's clan in the lucrative nightclubs they frequented.

But he'd left that part of his life behind.

Hopefully, it wouldn't come chasing after him.

The reinforcements Dalhu had asked for were due to arrive any day now. Navuh was sending a large contingent this time, and he had no doubt someone higher up in the organization would be leading them. Dalhu had been a commander of a small unit. There was no way he would've been left to head the operation, regardless of the fact that discovering Annani's clan's elusive trail had been his achievement.

Whatever, it was of no consequence. He had abandoned the Brotherhood and its questionable crusade for good.

Heading for the staircase, he paused and looked at the two top windows flanking the fireplace. The exposed glass made him uneasy.

All the other windows had shutters, which he'd closed, but those two at the top had none. If there had been a tall ladder he could've used, he would've taped or nailed bed sheets over the glass, but as he'd searched the cabin and the attached woodshed, the only ladder he'd found was too short.

Those windows were a dead giveaway that someone was inside the cabin, and even though it was unlikely that anyone would be looking for Amanda out here in the mountains, Dalhu hated taking even that slight chance.

He would have to insist on as little lighting as possible.

With a curse, he jogged down the stairs, his scowl deepening as he took in the pillow and blanket the princess had prepared for him on the couch. Not for a moment did he entertain the notion that she'd intended to sleep there herself. But if she thought he would be a gentleman and cram himself into the thing, she had another thing coming.

Spoiled brat...

A beautiful, sexy, spoiled brat...

Standing barefoot at the counter, Amanda was a vision—looking amazing even in the plain pink sweats he'd gotten her. The pants waistband, which was clearly too wide for her narrow waist, was rolled over a couple of times, and the loose pants hung low on her hips, allowing him a glimpse of the curve of her creamy white ass each time she bent.

And she'd made coffee and sandwiches…

Maybe there was hope for her after all.

"You are beautiful," Dalhu breathed as he walked up to stand behind her and nuzzled her long, smooth neck.

Surprised, she shivered before ducking sideways. "Cut it out, Dalhu," she bit out. "Sit down and drink your coffee. I hope you like it black and bitter because you didn't get any sugar or creamer."

"That's so sweet of you, taking care of me like that," he said as he sat down and picked up the coffee mug.

"Don't get used to that."

As Dalhu took a sip, he barely made it to the sink in time to spit the thing out. "Are you trying to poison me, woman? What the hell did you do?" He rushed back to the table, grabbing a peanut butter sandwich and taking a quick bite to get rid of the gritty taste.

"There is no coffeemaker, okay? What did you expect?" The hurt expression on Amanda's face made it obvious that she didn't ruin the coffee just to spite him. Grabbing the pot by the handle, she dumped its contents in the sink, then braced her hands on the rim and dropped her head. Her delicate shoulders began trembling.

Was she crying? Did he make her cry?

Way to go, asshole…

"Don't worry about it. I'll make a new one." He got behind her and tried to turn her around.

A sob escaped her throat as she shrugged his hands off her shoulders. "Everything you got from that store is disgusting; the towels, the bedding, the clothes… everything… even the food. The bread tastes like cardboard, and everything else is canned yuck. And now I can't even have a decent cup of coffee. It's just too much… I can't take it anymore…" She began sobbing in earnest.

Dalhu felt helpless. What the hell was he supposed to do now?

"Please don't cry. If you make me a list, I'll go and get you whatever you need. I'm sorry that there was nothing better at that general store... Oh, hell..." Forcing her to turn, he wrapped his arms around her, crushing her to him—her cheek to his pec.

She struggled, but he held her tightly against him, rubbing his palm over her heaving back until she gave up and sagged in his arms. Crying and sobbing into his sweatshirt for what seemed like forever, Amanda was killing him.

And although he was well aware that the coffee was just the last straw that had broken this strong, amazing woman, the guilt of failing to provide for her, like he'd promised her he would, was eating him alive.

As the sobbing subsided, he reached for a paper towel, and still holding her with one arm, handed her the thing.

"Thank you." Amanda hiccuped and blew her nose into the towel. Pushing away from him, she threw it into the sink and wiped her face with her sleeve before glancing up at him. "I must be a mess. Red nose and blotchy eyes..."

"You're beautiful. Always. In any shape or form." He dipped his knees to look into the blue pools of her eyes, wanting to kiss her so bad it hurt.

She smiled a little. "You're just saying it to make me feel better."

"No, I mean it. Come, sit down, relax, and I'll make you a good cup of coffee to cheer you up." He led her to the dining table and pulled out a chair for her.

"Good luck. There is no cream or sugar. So even if you manage to brew a decent coffee, I wouldn't like it."

"Oh, but you've missed something when you put the cans away. We have some condensed milk—it's both sweet and creamy."

ALSO BY I. T. LUCAS

DARK GUARDIAN CRAVED

DARK GUARDIAN'S MATE

DARK ANGEL

DARK ANGEL'S OBSESSION

DARK ANGEL'S SEDUCTION

DARK ANGEL'S SURRENDER

DARK OPERATIVE

DARK OPERATIVE: A SHADOW OF DEATH

DARK OPERATIVE: A GLIMMER OF HOPE

DARK OPERATIVE: THE DAWN OF LOVE

DARK SURVIVOR

DARK SURVIVOR AWAKENED

DARK SURVIVOR ECHOES OF LOVE

DARK SURVIVOR REUNITED

DARK WIDOW

DARK WIDOW'S SECRET

DARK WIDOW'S CURSE

DARK WIDOW'S BLESSING

DARK DREAM

DARK DREAM'S TEMPTATION

DARK DREAM'S UNRAVELING

DARK DREAM'S TRAP

DARK PRINCE

DARK PRINCE'S ENIGMA

DARK PRINCE'S DILEMMA

DARK PRINCE'S AGENDA

Dark Power Unleashed

Dark Power Convergence

DarkMemories

Dark Memories Submerged

Dark Memories Emerge

Dark Memories Restored

Dark Hunter

Dark Hunter's Query

Dark Hunter's Prey

Dark Hunter's Boon

Dark God

Dark God's Avatar

The Children of the Gods Series Sets

Books 1-3: Dark Stranger trilogy

Includes a bonus short story:

The Fates take a Vacation

Books 4-6: Dark Enemy Trilogy

Includes a bonus short story:

The Fates' Post-Wedding Celebration

Books 7-10: Dark Warrior Tetralogy

Books 11-13: Dark Guardian Trilogy

Books 14-16: Dark Angel Trilogy

Books 17-19: Dark Operative Trilogy

Books 20-22: Dark Survivor Trilogy

PERFECT MATCH

FOR EXCLUSIVE PEEKS AT UPCOMING RELEASES & A FREE COMPANION BOOK

Join my *VIP Club* and gain access to the VIP portal at itlucas.com

go to: http://eepurl.com/blMTpD

Included in your free membership:

- **FREE** Children of the Gods companion book 1
- **FREE** narration of Goddess's Choice—Book 1 in The Children of the Gods Origins series.
- Preview chapters of upcoming releases.
- And other exclusive content offered only to my VIPs.